WITH

WATERBORNE

JOANNE SOPER-COOK

Waterborne

GOOSE LANE

Edited by Laurel Boone.
Cover image: *Maiden Voyage* (detail) from The Mermaid Collection™
by Jason Gregory Gold, © 1994 Jason Gregory Gold. All Rights Reserved.
Cover and interior design by Julie Scriver.
Printed in Canada by Transcontinental Printing.
10 9 8 7 6 5 4 3 2 1

National Library of Canada Cataloguing in Publication Data

Soper-Cook, JoAnne
Waterborne

ISBN 0-86492-307-4

I. Title.
PS8587.O72W37 2002   C813'.54   C2002-900832-8
PR9199.3.S574W37 2002

Published with the financial support of the Canada Council for the Arts,
the Government of Canada through the Book Publishing Industry
Development Program, and the New Brunswick Culture and Sports Secretariat.

Goose Lane Editions
469 King Street
Fredericton, New Brunswick
CANADA E3B 1E5
www.gooselane.com

Once again, for Paul

*I'd like to thank my husband, Paul,
for his enduring support, and my editor,
Laurel Boone, whose tremendous insight and
knowledge, coupled with her diligent hard work,
made this novel what it is. I would also like to
thank Christine Hoffos, who read the book in
manuscript and offered many astute comments.*

CHAPTER ONE

I've had the dream twice now — once last night, and now tonight. It seems to be testing me, circling warily as if to gauge my readiness. I know it will come again.

I'm walking in the old road, the nether end of the path in Elsinore, when I meet my grandmother Bristow and various other mourners coming from the house. Nanny Bristow says, "We're going ta see yer mither," and in a flood of tears I proclaim, "Mother is dead."

And then I am in the basement of Nanny Bristow's house, her old house upon the hill at Elsinore. I know it is her house because as I approach, I see it looming as it often seemed to, a monument. But the basement isn't her basement — it's our house, from when I was a child, when we lived in that house with the unfinished basement and the gaps in the floor that leaked cold air into the house.

This basement of my childhood is filled with corpses, and among them is my mother. In the first dream, she is in a closed casket, but I know it's her because I can sense her, I can feel her living there as she has always done, just underneath my skin. She is ingrained in me, rubbed into me as a stain would be or a tattoo, and I can never efface that mark, that point of entry; my mother inhabits even the spaces behind my eyes. Tonight, she's lying in repose, covered in black satin, hands folded upon her chest and her eyes closed, although she might open them at any minute. She might sit up and speak to me. She looks as if she's sleeping, but I prefer to think she's dead. And the basement is half-filled with dark water, dirty and bilious, like filthy seawater from a shipwrecked bilge. The corpses are all afloat on this, as in a great womb, and something tells me, *This is your family*. Something tells me that all the women of my family are lying there, half-submerged in the dark basement, and drowned. My mother at last is dead.

The dream ends the way all unsettling dreams do: I reach across the expanse of my bed to touch the sheets, the eiderdown. My sleep-sodden mind conjures a fragment of a memory: *when someone is to die, you'll hear whistling in the night*. I fancy I can hear it now, like the birdcalls she used to imitate, telling me which bird was which and how they made their nests. I hear the whistling in the dark, and I know beyond a scintilla of doubt that my mother is already dead, because a voice whispers it inside my head.

And then the telephone is ringing, shattering my dream, revealing truth.

My name is Stella Goulding, Stella Maris Goulding, and I am what you might call locally famous. When I was eighteen years old, I left my home, a small Newfoundland outport with the fantastic name of Elsinore; I knew there was something else that would be better for me. I had no idea what this was — I had no idea about anything in those days. I suppose I expected what everybody expects at that age: to go out and make my mark upon the world in grand style. Nobody ever told me that the world is made of mighty hard stuff and resists most marks with a resilience that would put diamond to shame. I was awfully young then, and I figured that I knew it all. I would go someplace exotic, like St. John's, and get a job writing advertising copy, like F. Scott Fitzgerald, and I would wait to be discovered. No, that's not quite right. I don't think I had any really developed notions of being a writer back then — I only wanted something that would bring me the greatest amount of fame or notoriety with the least amount of work and that would come bundled with wealth of some significant portion.

You didn't get to see fame or wealth in Elsinore, and I can't honestly say that we had more than the usual share of notoriety. Darrel Hunt was caught one summer taking little Judie Fifield's clothes off out behind his father's woodshed; what he intended to do with the clothes once he had got them off is anybody's guess. It did not bear thinking that he intended any harm to Judie, for he had never been known to lay a finger on a living soul. Nevertheless, Headley Tucker and Anson Short were sick and tired of chasing him out of Headley's father's garage, where Darrel used to like to stand around listening to the boys talking bullshit and looking at the dirty pictures in the calendar on Headley's father's wall.

I wanted more than that, only I had no real idea what it was. It wasn't as if anyone ever expected anything of me, at least not anything spectacular. Nanny Bristow figured I would make my own way after a fashion, and Father never said anything at all.

The ringing phone tears me from the nest of sleep. I reach for it, jiggle the receiver from the cradle and hold it tenderly before me, dangling it by the cord. In the silence I am listening to it, listening to the sound of someone breathing, and the deeper noise behind it: the penetrating hum of the wires, the intermittent crackle of electricity or static. The sound is not a sound at all but a distance, the hiss of time bent back upon itself. I imagine it is the kind of sound that stretches between the stars in space, an invisible web. "Hello?"

"He's gone. The old man is gone. Won't be back no more, no."

A click, the breaking of a thread, and she is gone again, popping out of existence. Her voice sounds different, as if I expected that she would be dead; she can't be dead, though, because she has spoken to me. Perhaps she exists in an eternal present, the thickening swath of the *now*, caught up in great, sweeping loops between the moments. I am never sure what regions she inhabits. I think she might be slightly mad, but I cannot be certain; when I try to form a clear image of her face I fail, and I imagine that she sheds her skin from time to time as selkies do.

I turn the bedside clock to face me, and, squinting at it, I am able to discern that it is eleven-thirty. I went to bed early, feeling certain that if I stayed awake this evening the urge for it would come back, and I could not trust myself with what was in the house: all those cans and bottles, plastic packages and cardboard boxes. I always start out by pretending that I'm not going to do it, or that I can try something and it won't make any difference, but I should know better now. I can't stop it taking over like it does, and then I forget everything and try to pretend it doesn't matter. I can throw the evidence away and almost convince myself that I wasn't the one who did it, but of course there is always the other thing to do. I only ever use the one knife for that, and I only ever allow myself to make three or four long cuts — sometimes five, but no more. It's too easy for it to get away from me, and I don't want an infection. I don't want visits to the doctor and having to explain again, like when the dentist looked in my mouth and asked questions. Three or four long cuts are enough, and I can strap it up myself afterwards. Poppy Bristow used to say, *What the eyes don't see, the heart don't feel*. The heart only feels what's right in front of your face. Perhaps this is why I can ignore my mother's existence for astonishing stretches.

My God, Nanny Bristow. When I was a little girl in Elsinore, Nanny Bristow was the one person I could always count on. She was from what Mother called the Old Country, which meant she was from

Scotland. I had never been to Scotland, had only seen pictures of it in books and such, and it wasn't until I got older and had some money to travel that I saw it first-hand. There was a stench of diesel fuel in the air, North Sea petrol, they called it, and everything was a mad rush. I took the train at Waverley Station and went down to London, because I was a lot braver in those days, and I never thought there was anything to fear from anybody. I could go any-where and do anything and no one would ever bother me. It was a different world to me then. The whole of it was waiting there, uncut, like a lovely fresh orange, and I had all the time there was. In St. John's, I wished my days away until the weekend, when I could get aboard the bus and go back home to Elsinore: four and a half hours if there was no traffic and the roads were clear.

Nanny Bristow was the centre of my world back then. I knew the other children didn't have a grandmother like mine, that Nanny was different, that she knew things the other nannies didn't know. She would wait for me at the end of the path, and when I got off the school bus, we would return together to her house and a table set for afternoon tea. "I'm sure my mother is losing her mind," my mother said, the remark directed not toward me so much as through me. "Makin' up tea like that for a youngster. She's cracked, sure."

I loved Nanny Bristow's teas. She would have sweet bread cut very thin and spread with real butter (my mother fed us margarine because it was so cheap) and tea in delicate bone china cups, patterned with violets or roses and edged with gold. "You drink up yer tea, there's a guid girrul," she'd say to me, in that gentle burr that she had never lost in fifty years. She had a pair of little bronze or brass bells in the shape of Highland terriers, which I would polish carefully with Brasso when I spent weekends at her house, and she would ring one of these to summon me to the tea table. I would hide out in one of the other rooms or pretend to be upstairs so she could ring and I would come running. It was such a taste of luxury to sit at the table with a linen napkin in my lap and eat sweet bread cut so thin you could see the daylight through it. My mother always said, "I don't know why my mother cuts the bread like that for. She's too cheap to feed ye properly." Her criticism annoyed me. I wondered what she had to complain about, but such trivialities never bothered Mother.

Mother complained like other people drank water: regularly, daily, unstintingly. When I realised the truth, much later on, I concluded that she just really liked to hear the sound of her own voice — that it was some kind of tonic for her, a restorative, the way some people's souls gladden at the sound of church bells. Mother would complain about the weather, the music on the radio, the mud in the path coming up to the house, the way Doreen Short's clothes were hung on the line, the way the string coiled down from the ceiling of Fifield's store and made a dirty grey puddle on the counter, like the strings of old mops . . . on and on and on, forever and ever, world without end, amen amen. Perhaps I should have learned to tune her out, but there was no way to tune my mother out: her voice, rising and falling, followed me everywhere throughout the house, a constant din like rain upon a metal roof. *Blessed be to Jesus, let the hallelujahs roll if that youngster comes in this g.d. house once more the day asking for stuff I'm going to run away I can't sit down and git a minute's peace but she's always in here asking for something and wanting a drink of water or wanting something to eat and look at the dirt look at the mud what in the name of the world is wrong with you anyway and don't look at me like that and take that look right off your face right now my dear I don't have to put up with a puss like that on you where's your mitts where's your scarf did you brush your teeth go and wash your filthy paws you dirty god-blessed thing the day here I am working me arse off scoating me guts out not that you appreciates it because you don't oh no and one of these days I'll be dead and gone and in the ground and you'll tink no more of me than if I was nailed agin the wall.* I was always astonished, and am now, that she could keep it up, seemingly without pausing to draw breath. She would often

12

wander off into another room of the house, and her voice would die away slightly, like a radio that has somehow drifted off its station. Then abruptly, as she moved back within range, her voice would crescendo, peak and then vanish, as if someone had turned her off. I have never heard a performance like it, and it has stayed with me; sometimes late at night, on the edge of sleep, I hear her, just around the rim of my mind, and I feel as if I'm nine years old again. *Don't look at me like that you dirty little scunner or you'll be laughing out the other side of your mouth and that you will I'm ashamed to be seen with ye like something nobody owns and what have you got that on for?*

I would lie awake in the dark for a long time, willing her voice away.

I don't know what to do now that the old man is gone. It's not like he was ever here much, even when he was alive, sure. And now there's no sense sitting up with a candle in the window or a lamp on the table or all the electric on, waiting for him. He's not coming back no more. He's gone for good.

Joss was over the day and split up some wood for me. Thank God I got Joss to depend on, anyway. Not like that other lazy cunt out to St. John's ever comes in this way to see if I needs anything or if I'm laid out dead on the floor. Thank God I got Joss to depend on. I can't do for myself and I never could. He fills up the woodbox for me and brings me a pail of water from the old spring up behind my mother's house, the good water. Right out of the rock it is, just so clear as anything and right sweet to drink. I wouldn't make me tea with nothing else.

I had Joss in to the house for a cup of tea the day. The old man is laid out up to Marion's place — I wouldn't have en in here. I know it's not right, but I can't stand it, me nerves are not good, I got bad nerves. I'd be frightened to death he'd sit up and talk to me, and I can't stand it. So the men came from the church and carried en over to Marion's house. She'll lay en out. She knows what to do. I don't know what to do. Me nerves are just about gone with it. I had to phone *her* in to St. John's and tell her that her father was dead. Sure, she wouldn't bother to pick up the phone. I could drop off the face of the earth, my dear, and she wouldn't bother to come and see me. I don't understand it, I never did understand it, why she turned her back on her father and me. I don't understand it, although I suppose it's like it says in the Bible about youngsters rising up agin their parents in the Last Days.

She was never right in the head. I don't know what we done to her for her to turn out like that, I don't know. Sure, I never done no less for her than my mother done for me. She went in there to St. John's and got in with that crowd at the university, and she was never the same after, that's what I says happened, as sure as I'm here the day. "You reads too many books," I said to her, yes, and that's what I did. "You reads that old foolishness and fills up your head with old garbage." Her father would have said it to her if he was around. I knowed he would have.

Marion will have en all laid out and dressed by the morrow. I might go up and see en. I should go up and see en, I suppose. I don't know how I feels about it or how I'm supposed to feel about it, him being dead. I thought for sure he'd die out on the water like they all do. I thought he'd go like old Uncle Wins, out on the fishing grounds in a gale. They says Uncle Wins never learned how to swim, he was that scared of getting took overboard. They says it's better not to know how, if you'm going out on the water.

I wouldn't want to go out on the water. I don't want nothing to do with it, I'm afraid of it, and that's the truth. No sir, you can have that for me. I minds when my father used to go out in the spring after the seals, out on the ice. I could never stand to kill a animal, I knows that. I'm too soft-hearted, I couldn't do it. I likes a bit of seal meat, though, or a bit of flipper pie. That one in to St. John's, she won't eat it, says it's filthy. There's nothing in the world better for ye than a good bit of seal, sure. And the skin makes a lovely coat. I had a sealskin coat made for Stella when she was a baby, up to Trepassey, was a man up there used to make them by hand, and all the stitching so lovely and fine. Gone to get a selkie skin, to put the baby bunting in . . . is that the way it goes? That's what my mother used to sing to me when I was small: *gone to get a selkie skin to wrap the baby bunting in*.

I'll have to go up to Marion's the morrow to see en. God forgive me, he's me husband. I can't believe he's gone, just like that, dropped down dead in the middle of the floor, eating a lassie bun with his cup of tea. I suppose I'll cry later on, I might. Thank God there's no one else to tell. Thank God my mother only ever had me and stopped with one.

I'm right glad of Joss, though. He's some good.

I am here for the funeral; I am home again. This is the one place whose every feature is impressed upon my memory so that I could never forget it, even if I wanted to. Today, the hills and valleys, the longitudinal sweep of the cove are as manifest and real to me as if I had carved them with my own hands. After all this time, I still feel as if I own them, as if they are truly mine.

It is snowing fitfully, in spits and shivers, a hard, grainy snow that feels like icy sand against the face, the hands. My mother stands across from me, and we are separated by the abyss that is my father's open grave. She is wearing the ratty old fur coat that Nanny Bristow brought from Fife all those years ago, the one that Auntie Mavis tried to steal and hide under Great-Grandmother's bed. My father hated that coat — when Mother wore it, he said it looked as if it were sewn together out of mouse pelts. Does her wearing it today, of all days, mean something in particular? Does it hint at a textured underside that I have missed? Things shift and change when you least expect them to. Life is by no means certain.

I watch my mother carefully, never looking directly at her but looking past her as I have trained myself to do. I cannot allow myself to catch her eye, even if I force myself to gaze into her face. I can bear to scrutinize her features only when her attention is occupied elsewhere, when she is not looking at me. She looks the same as always: the long dark hair, as shiny as if it had been lacquered, pulled up on the sides and pinned underneath the black velour hat she wears. Her lips are tight, compressed below her pointed nose. Her eyelids have begun to sag, and I wonder if this is how I will look when I am her age. It is still a lovely face — indeed, the loveliest woman's face I have ever seen — and more lovely still for all that it is so remote, the face that has turned away from me at least a thousand times since I was born. She reminds me of the woman atop the wedding cake: serene and featureless but lovely in memory, as if she managed somehow to draw every human beauty to herself.

Between us now there is my father, safe inside his casket. I wonder if the dead can hear the living, or if the ears are clotted up and deafened when the brain cuts its final moorings. What would he think of it all? He was so stolid, so stoic and strangely resolute, plodding his way through life like a beast in harness. I wish I had known him better, except that he was never around for me to know, and no one can undo what's done, especially not me. It's difficult enough keeping myself grounded in the everyday.

I brought something with me just to keep me stable. I always make sure to take care of myself that way because I could never think of going into one of the shops here and getting what I needed. It would be like buying cigarettes or condoms — everybody would know all about it in under five minutes: *Mim Goulding's girl was in here the day buying rubbers.* I always carry an extra-large purse, like a tote bag, really, so I can keep whatever I need in there. Depending on how things go today, I might not need it at all. I'm hoping I won't need it. I don't like to fall back on it if I'm away from home because I never know if I can find a comfortable spot to do what needs to be done. I've got that as well, an X-Acto knife with a piece of cork on it. I couldn't possibly leave the house without taking what I need. It just gets too tense, and I never know how Mother will react, what kind of fuss she'll cause. Best to be prepared.

They put my father in the ground. I try not to think of anything at all, but even I'm not as disciplined as that, so I remember him the last time I saw him, getting down into the boat one morning, turning around to wave at me. I try to have only good memories of him, but truthfully, I don't really have any memories at all. I can recall hardly anything except a few stray bits and crumbs of him from when I was very small, and even those feel oddly distorted, strange and far away. I think about the wood stove that stood just inside the living room in our house at Elsinore, and Mother feeding sticks of wood into it, and Father home from the Labrador or home from somewhere, lying on the daybed with his arms crossed behind his head, listening to the news. The wood stove gave out such an intense heat that even sitting across the room from it, my eyes felt hot. I cannot be certain this memory is real because whenever I recall it, it retains the nebulous aspect of a daydream. These are the only memories I have of him, the only memories I need.

They aren't supposed to lower the casket with all of us standing here, not really. It seems improper to stare at it going down the hole, and so I lift my gaze a little.

Uncle Joss and Mother, smiling in a particular way across my father's open grave. I think he winks at her. I think it is him she is smiling at. I know I will have to take care of myself as soon as I can get somewhere and be alone. I knew I brought all of it with me for a reason.

We got the old man put in the ground. I can't say I'm glad to see en gone, but that's the way it is, I suppose. Not much I can do about it. Sure, what am I going to do? Bring en back again?

Nita Fifield came over after they had en put down and said, *You're in our prayers, Miz Goulding.* I knowed she never meant it. She thinks just because I goes over to the church sometimes on a Sunday night that I'm religious.

We buried en in the old graveyard over on the hill, where all the Gouldings are buried and where I expect I'll be buried, too, by and by. The Bristows are buried over to the United cemetery, down by the harbour. They don't like to mix with the other crowd, although I don't see what difference it makes after you'm dead. I wouldn't say that out loud, now. People got some queer ideas about dying and all that, with religion all mixed up into it. I don't really care one way or the other.

Joss was up to the house when I was getting ready to go to the funeral. He come up around nine o'clock, just after I got the bed made, and said it wouldn't be right for me to be going to me husband's funeral all by myself. He took the new truck, even though I know he'd rather have walked, since it's not that far along. He come in just as I was putting me hat on, that black one that Marion gave to me last Christmas. I shouldn't say this, but I was right glad to see en. I always liked Joss, even after what happened years ago. He's not so tall as Jack was, he's kind of short, and he got a bit of a gut on en, starting to lose his hair and that, but he got a nice face, like. Nice blue eyes. I wonder if that's where Stella gets it to.

I'd like to died at en over to the graveyard, honest to God. Here I am, standing there with Stella on the other side of it, looking out over my shoulder like she always done (she never looks me in the face, I don't know what's wrong with that girl), and Joss over there, winking at me.

I had a dress when I was fourteen, a dress that Noreen Francis made for me for Speech Night up to the school. It was pale blue taffeta, with a powder blue underskirt and a crinoline made out of net. Nobody else had a dress like it, Noreen took this sewing course through the mail from down the States and was right good at doing up dresses. All the boys lined up against the wall to dance with me, and I looked some nice. I know I looked nicer than the rest, nobody had a dress like that.

I don't know why Stella is the way she is. I saw her looking when Joss winked at me. Of course she knows better than to say anything to me, I'd smack the mouth off her. She's not too old for that, let me tell you. I'm fed up with her anyhow. She turned away from everything we taught her and went her own way, even though she knew it was wrong. She knows what's right, we taught her what was right, and all I hears is her on television and the radio, talking about what kinds of books she's writing, old garbage. She would have done better for herself if she married Harry Bailey when he wanted her, but no, she was too good for that. I don't bother with her. I knows her phone number if I needs to get hold of her, and I knows where she lives, out back of St. John's. Topsail, it's called — that place with all the nice trees. I won't bother with her, though. She humiliated her father and me by talking about the church on television, saying that we was hard to her when she was growing up. It didn't even look like Stella now, and that's the truth. She changed that much, got her hair dyed dark and makeup on her eyes like a hoor. I won't be reading any of her books, I can tell you that. She was always reading when she was small, I couldn't get her out of the house supposing it was hot enough to burn a hole in ye. "What's that you're reading, Stella?" I used to say to her. "Words," she'd tell me. Saucy as a black, she was. Of course, I think my mother taught her that — up to my mother's house all the time after school, sot down to the table having tea as fancy as ye please and my mother filling her head with foolishness about going to Scotland when she was finished with school. I suppose my mother figured she'd go over there and live with them two lizzies. I'm ashamed to say it about my mother's own sister, but it's true. Her and that other one, lizzies, both of 'em, living together in Glasgow. Yes, I know I'd let Stella go over there with the like of that.

It's no odds now, anyway. She got her life ruined. She'll never get a husband. Sure, what man wants that? A woman hid away in a room at the typewriter all day long, making up lies about people. That's all she does, makes up lies. Every bit of it is lies. There's no man wants the like of that. He wants youngsters to carry on his name, and a home, and something on the table in the nighttime that's fit to eat. That's all Jack ever wanted, and that's what I gave en till the day he died. I never opened me mouth about what went on with Joss, and there was no reason for Jack to know. He married me because he wanted me for his wife, and there was no call for anyone to say anything about Stella, not to Jack. He accepted her because he didn't know no better.

I don't care what she thinks now. I'm finished with her. She can get back on her high horse and go on back to St. John's or Topsail or wherever she likes. I don't care what she does. She's no daughter of mine.

I think I'll go up to the graveyard now next week and see if they got en all squared away right. I likes looking at the names on the headstones up there. Most of the people that stays in Elsinore now are dead. Everybody else is getting out.

I think about things while I wind the gauze around my wrist. I've gotten so good at it that I can do without tape — tie a knot in the ends of it with my teeth. I am strangely proud of this. I was able to slip back to the house before Mother came home from the cemetery, thank God, and lock myself in the bathroom. Of course years ago we didn't even have a bathroom as such, just a slop bucket on the floor in that other bedroom upstairs, the one with the really cold walls and the window that was always frosted over in winter. Dear God, it was cold in there. I remember it as if it were yesterday: pulling down my pants and sitting on the cold enamel edge of it, smelling the mingled scents of Lysol and piss, the residual odour of old shit and sodden Kleenex. Trying to sit on just the edge of it, so as not to tip the damned thing like I did one night, tipped it so that it over-turned. As luck and the devil would have it, it was full. The contents overspilled the bedroom floor and coursed into the hollow walls. I remember the yellow streaks of piss, drying into my mother's Old Rose wallpaper. It came out in patches for months thereafter, some brown, some yellow, until the ruined paper began to pull away from the wall. I hadn't tried to do it — it was an acci-dent, I had simply sat too far forward on the brimming bucket and it succumbed to gravity. I remember Mother wailing about it: *I can't have nothing, look, that g.d. youngster is so dirty as a pig and can't do nothing without making a god-blessed filthy slut of herself and here I am now up to me arse in shite and what in the name of the world did you think you were doing? What?*

The memory shouldn't give me pleasure, but it does. I'm sure Freud or Jung would have much to say. I don't doubt there's a theory about it, smearing the matriarchal breast with shit or whatever. Some ivory tower feminazi in woolly tights has doubtless formulated an explanation for why I hate my mother so much. I'm sure of it, I know people are paid and indeed make their living deciphering just such mysteries as these.

I keep having the dream, even when I'm not thinking about her, even when she's the farthest thing from my mind. I can be working away happily, without fear of interruption, and I can go to bed, suitably sated by whatever means necessary, and she will be there, rearing out of my dreams, my own monster. In my sleep I see her at the end of my upstairs hallway, belting her housecoat around her like a suit of armour, preparing to do battle, her lips compressed and thin, taut with disapproval.

Or else I will dream of her as she was before me: the belle of the ball, the pretty girl that everybody danced with, a sylph in a pale blue dress. She is unconscious of my presence because I have not come to her just yet; she is still untainted by me. She has not been marked, not yet. That particular humiliation will come later. I will come later.

I told my mother nothing. Instead I told it all to Nanny Bristow, but even she could not get close to me, was not permitted to touch me as children are touched. She tried to teach me how to knit once and sat behind me with her arms about me, and I had to excuse myself on the pretext of going to the bathroom so I could run and close the door behind me and weep into the towels, then wash my face and hands and come back to her, pick up the stitches where I'd left them. I couldn't stand it with her arms around me; it made me cry, and crying would never do. Crying infuriated Mother most of all. *I'll give you something to cry about, my dear.* It simply wasn't done. Better to keep it all inside, smother the agony until it felt like dying, like choking or swallowing a sticky ball that wouldn't go down no matter how hard I glutched. She hated it when I cried: *Your face all screwed up like that, you looks like a hen's hole.*

I got run over by a car when I was young, eleven years old or eight or nine, I don't remember. I recall the heat of the exhaust burning into my forehead, lying under the machine and seeing the dark underbelly coming closer, listening to the crunch of wheels and not daring to cry out because I knew that if I made so much as a sound she would kill me. It was an odd scene. *I got run over by a car.* Standing in the doorway with the knee torn out of my slacks and a crescent-shaped burn already puffed into a blister in the very centre of my forehead. *Mother, I got run over.* I think she was in the bathroom. I remember standing in the middle of the floor and calling out for her, bleating like small animals do: *Ma-a-a-am.* She told me never to call her that, I was to call her Mother, and especially in company.

Her hands were wet, she'd been washing in the bathroom, her shiny dark hair loose in a gorgeous coil about her neck. I wanted to touch it, to smooth it between my fingers, but I knew that was expressly forbidden. She preferred that I did not touch her; she didn't like it, she said. *What in the name of God are you blarin' out like that for? What?*

I got run over by a car.

Well you're not dead, are ye? Go and wash your dirty mouth. You looks like the wrath of God.

Mother always said that Nanny Bristow was nuts. "My mother's gone all together now," she'd say. "She's gone right off the head, sure." She would tell anyone who'd listen: *My mother I'm sure is half-cracked. Cracked, sure. Loony tunes.* But then she'd phone Nanny Bristow religiously every single morning and call her Ma and croon and simper for her on the phone. Whenever she needed anything at all, she went to Nanny, because Father was away at sea, and there was really no one else to whom she might appeal for help. It was doubtful that Father's family — Uncle Joss, Aunt Marion, Aunt Eleanor who was in the madhouse then, shrieking like the bells of Hell — would have anything to do with her. There was no one to whom she could preen and simper except Nanny. It was unthinkable that she not preen and simper. I do believe it was what she was put upon this earth to do. Perhaps I'm being cruel. No, I think I am being truthful.

My mother had the TB in her spine in the fifties, when everybody just about in Elsinore was coming down with it. She went over to Boyce Fifield's and drunk some milk from one of his cows, and old Mrs. Fifield, Boyce's mother, never bothered to scald it on the stove first. She was a bit slutty, Mrs. Fifield; she used to let stuff slide, you could say, around the house and that. If you went down there, sure, you had to force your way in through the door, there was that much old rubbish around. You could stir the bloody place with a stick.

My mother ended up in the San for two years, lying on the broad of her back. I was fourteen when she got sick, I'll never forget it. When my father told me, I ran up to the bedroom and bawled and bawled, because I thought for sure she was going to die. I told Eva, "I'm not going to have either mother." I was really frightened, and I don't mind telling you. Of course, she wasn't around much when I was small, she had to go to work in to the old General in St. John's. My father never made much money at the fish. She used to go away on Sunday night on the bus and come home Friday evening. She sometimes used to bring us stuff from the Arcade, down on Water Street. Once I got a pair of earrings that clipped on because she didn't agree with young girls having their ears pierced, she said it was hoorish. Them earrings, I can see 'em right now in my mind's eye, they looked like pearls, just like real pearls, and you'd never know the difference. I kept 'em in me top drawer, and I remember I lost one at the Christmas dance out to the Lodge when I was sixteen. Just about broke my heart, so it did. I never wore earrings after I got married to Jack because he wasn't raised to it. He said it was prideful for a woman to have herself all done up like that with holes in her ears and makeup on. He said if the Lord had meant for women to have earrings, he would've give us long bits of skin hanging down from our ears and we could paint 'em different colours. Jack said some queer things sometimes.

She used to go away and work in to the Old General when I was small, and my father used to be up at the fish right early in the morning, so I'd do a little bit around the house before I went to school — wash the clothes and make up the beds, clean the vege-tables for supper or put a bit of fish in to soak, things like that. When I got home from school in the evening, I could start the supper while I did the rest of the house, and I had it done then. I'd try and have something ready for my mother when she came home on Fridays from St. John's. My father always liked a bit of fish on Fridays, even though we belonged to the United Church, so I'd have that with a few scruncheons and a bit of drowned butter.

She went into the San, though, for two years, lying on the broad of her back. She used to write me letters when she worked in to the old General, and on Thursday nights, after my bath, my father would let me call her on the phone and talk to her if she wasn't working the night shift. She had a room in on Forest Road with a couple other nurses, they all stayed there together. I remember how the phone sounded when I'd call her up, right far away like you were calling down into a hole. She always told me to be a good girl, but she said it in Scotch, like, *Be a guid girrul*. The teacher I had for grade two said I was a half-breed because my mother was from Britain. I don't think she knew very much. Sure, it wasn't like Robert Tucker's crowd, and he married to an Indian he got up to Nova Scotia, a Micmac. A half-breed, yes, I minds now. I don't think very many in Elsinore knew what the inside of a book looked like, and that one was as bad as all the rest, even though she was a teacher. Thank God I had the television when Stella was small or I would have been drove off me head. I had to push her out the door in the morning so she'd go off and play. She was never one for the other youngsters, they used to torment her all the time. I told her, "You got to stick up for yourself. Sure, you're as soft as shite." The other ones picked on her, flicking rocks at her and stuff like that. Sure, youngsters does that anyway. And I told her, "They picks on you because you cries. You gives em a reason to do it." She never listened to me, no more than if I was the man in the moon. I don't know what in the name of God was ever wrong with that youngster. Now that I thinks about it, she might have been a bit soft in the head, like Jack's crowd, like Eleanor, who spent time in the Mental. Stella was always right queer around other people, she never had nothing to say for herself, she'd sit behind my chair whenever anyone came to the house. I remember once this woman came along selling some kind of religious books. I figured I should buy something from her, because she was kind of poor-looking, one of those people.

Stella was there in the sitting room when she came along, I'll never forget it. She had on this old top she got from my mother, some kind of tartan thing that was all tore underneath the arms, and a pair of them stretchy slacks, way too big for her, they were. My mother had took her up to the beauty parlour the day before and got all her hair chopped off. Mind now, Stella never had good hair from the start of it, it wasn't wavy like mine, it was straight, straight as a whip, just like Eleanor's, like Jack's crowd. Her hair was all chopped off right short like a boy, with a fringe straight across her forehead like a Chinese. She come skulking into the room and glommed onto me, my dear, like I was the Water of Life. I don't know what in the name of the world she was into, but she had food colouring all over her hands, red and blue. If I told her once not to touch the god-blessed stuff, I told her a thousand times, but she never listened. I could talk to her sometimes and it was like she was off in a daydream. And she'd never look straight at me, either. I don't know what she was afraid of, sure I wasn't going to do anything to her.

Anyway, here's this poor woman going through the whole thing they goes through when they're selling stuff, posters spread out on the floor, and Stella is there, hiding behind my chair like she normally do, and God strike me down if she don't start fooling around with my hair while I'm there trying to talk to this woman. I could have smacked the mouth off her, twirling and twiddling around with it, and I told her before not to lay her dirty paws on it. I'm trying to talk to the woman, and Stella is there scraping and scrawbing at me like a little baby. I was that mad, I could have belted her one. "Go on out and play," I told her. "Stuck in the house listening to the grown-ups talking. You're always stuck to my arse, sure. Haven't you got any friends of your own?" I never had a minute's peace with her. I used to have to bawl out at her to get her to behave, and to tell you the God's truth, her skulking around the house all the time gave me the creeps, now God forgive me for saying it. I'd lie down on the chesterfield and try to get a nap, and she'd prop herself up there in front of me and stare at me with an expression on her face like nothing you ever saw. I can't even think about it, it gives me the creeps that bad. I have nightmares about it, her standing up there in front of me like that. I'd try to close my eyes and ignore her, like, and she'd still be there, I could hear her breathing. I never got no rest. I used to try and lie down around three o'clock, and honest to my God, it was like she knew. If she was anywhere in the house she'd come out and stand up there in front of the chesterfield and gawp at me. I always said that youngster wasn't right in the head. "Is you asleep, Mother?" she used to say. She knew bloody well I was trying to get a wink. "Mother, is you asleep?" And she'd keep asking it until she nearly drove me off me rocker. If I never had the television, I would have gone off me head and that's the truth. The youngster had no more imagination than fly in the air, and she was forever pestering me, whining and complaining. I don't hold with youngsters being brought up to be sooks, always tissing and bawling around their mother. I never sooked around my mother, I can tell you that. She wouldn't put up with it, no sir. I didn't let Stella do it, either. I wasn't having it, a youngster like that. It was all bad enough, Stella the way she was.

Yes, my mother went into the San for two years when I was young — the Sanatorium, that's what it was, for the TB patients. And when she come home out of it, she had to walk with two canes. They put her in a body cast that she had to have on all the time, and she couldn't sit up or lie down unless I helped her. My God, that was some bad. She couldn't do nothing around the house, and I had to help her. I was glad it was in the summertime, so at least I didn't have to worry about school, even though my mother always said I was as stun as your arse, that I probably wouldn't get nowhere. She used to say she should have stayed in Scotland, and then maybe I might have got a decent education instead of being taught in the little school in Elsinore. I couldn't do my times tables, and she used to try and help me with it, but I couldn't understand it. I could read really good, though, and do sums. My mother used to say I was never that bright: *You dinnae hae brains enough ta blow yer nose.* I don't know why she said stuff like that for. She was kind of hard when she got out of the San. I shouldn't say nothing bad about her, I suppose, she's my mother after all.

I don't know what I would have done if I had another youngster like Stella. Thank God she was the only one. I don't think I could have stood it.

If I were Jewish and she were dead, I could at least sit Shiva for my mother, but I have no such recourse. I keep no pictures of her in my house, you understand; I don't think I could endure any image of her staring at me from some obligingly supportive surface, the mantel or a wall. I have tried to make her dead to me, but it never works quite the way I imagine it will. I can always hear her voice somehow, the way it shrivelled me as a child, or she comes to me in dreams. I can garner no peace at all with her in my thoughts.

The dance always changes; she pulls me close and pushes me away with the same hand.

It is always a pleasure to get away from Elsinore. Whether I am back there for three hours or three days, the same sense of freedom washes over me as soon as I climb into my car and leave it behind me. The funeral was mercifully brief, and they put my father into the ground with a minimum of fuss and bother. As I drive away, I think about my mother and my Uncle Joss, that smile exchanged across my father's open grave, and, not for the first time, I wonder what it means. No, this is not entirely truthful: I know what it means. What I wonder at is that I am not surprised at all, that my mother has lost the capacity to shock me, when only a few years before a mere touch from her, the slightest breath of disapproval, and I would crumble into ashes.

I have always admired the way Elsinore looks in the rear-view mirror of my car, vanishing into the distance, becoming smaller and smaller until nothing is to be seen of it but a greasy smudge on the horizon. I believe it looks its best when seen from such an inverted perspective, as if whoever designed the place arranged it incorrectly, a flipped photograph, the mole on the chin on the right side instead of on the left. I have always been enthralled with inconsistencies such as these, the low, scrubby hills of Elsinore, for instance, slouching wearily towards the sea. It always seems to be such a tired place, weary of seeing its own faded face in the mirror of the ocean; it wishes we would all turn away for the moment it needs to don another aspect, but its moments are millennia, and besides, no one cares. Elsinore is Elsinore.

Topsail, just outside of St. John's, is the sort of town that prides itself on retaining whatever its original features might have been. It is neither large nor small and strangely homogenous: a glittering scrape of ocean rimmed with a pebble beach, the obligatory hills, a disinterested sky. I imagine that people think it a pretty little place, and were I able to regard it objectively at all, I would most likely agree. I like the trees, the ocean and the hills. I like the fact that it is far away from Elsinore. I am comforted by the idea that no one in Topsail knows me, or that anyone who does has the decency and character not to mention it. I am grateful for small favours such as these.

My books earn enough that I am able to live on what I make, a situation so unlikely for a writer here that I might have horns. I own a house, a white bungalow of some indeterminate style that I purchased with the proceeds from my first novel's movie option; its most satisfying feature is that it has a sturdy door, both front and back, that lock me in. It is unlike my mother's house, and perhaps I chose it for just that reason. There is no entrance directly into the living room, nor is there a narrow hallway with a door that partitions me from the rest of the dwelling as if I were a leper or some malefactor accused of crimes beyond the normal way of things. There are no tiny windows through which I squeeze on afternoons in summer, when Mother lies sleeping in the bedroom, breathing clouds of rummy vapour into the still air. There is no mouldy basement, no slick concrete floor with a perimeter of little waxy mushrooms. There is no sound of slow footsteps overhead, echoing off the plywood floor; nor do I hear the caustic, deliberate hack that Mother makes when she is retching in the bathroom. Perhaps this is where I learned it first: dry saltines in the morning and a glass of grapefruit juice in those days when everybody believed in the powers of grapefruit as they believed in Jesus. A glass of grapefruit juice and several crackers, leg lifts on the morning floor with sunshine coming through the windows. I would hide behind the partition in the dining room and watch her, swinging each leg in turn into the air, slimming her hips, she said. She had a lovely figure, my mother did: the long, curved legs of a dancer and a dancer's slender waist, graceful arms and hands, a wealth of glistening, shiny-dark hair. No wonder Aunt Marion and Aunt Eleanor hated her, and how she must have shamed them into righteous self-examination, these ugly sisters. I recall the wedding picture, my mother weeping beautifully, so very lovely, and I wonder where the softness in her face went. I wonder if anything can bring it back again, or if her smoothness and her roundness are gone forever — dried up, desiccated, shrivelled in the furnace blast of anger. I pride myself that I am not ignorant of what made my mother the way she is, nor am I unacquainted with the multi-layered tenets of my own faith. Knowing truth does not alter truth — at least, this is what I have always believed.

As soon as I get home, I turn on the television, flipping through all the channels to get to CNN. As far as news goes, I find that I must keep abreast of everything; if some major human drama occurs, no matter in what futile corner of existence, I must be a witness. It is important to expose myself to that strange space between pieties; only then can I see humanity for what it really is. Only then can I regard myself within my own essential sphere — disconnected, exiled, a being out of joint. Today there is another schoolyard shooting in the States, and someone has been discovered at the border near Seattle, trying to smuggle gunpowder into Canada or something like that. I flip through the channels, faster and faster, anxious to get at the core of everything before the images vanish and I am alone again. I imagine that the world will end as I have always expected: some kind of holocaust, Armageddon, a plague creeping over the face of nations like rot. I'm relieved that I have no children, that I never found a man I liked well enough to reproduce with. I never found anyone who held my interest.

I find myself thinking about my mother again, that covert look exchanged with Uncle Joss, and I must go down below, take the key from beside the basement door and let myself into the lair. Whenever I can't sleep I come down here, revel in the sight of it. The gleaming cans with their neat labels, the heat-sealed cardboard boxes and the glistening bottles reassure me; I arrive here as a supplicant before an oracle, hungry for some small intimacy with my Mother-God, the face of the Divine.

I allow myself the luxury of counting them: each row along the shelves horizontally, then multiplying vertically, then going one by one to make sure I haven't missed anything. While I am doing this I visualise how it will be: the trees and grass bending under a hellish firestorm, houses exploding, the ground humming with heat, until the shock wave arrives with a thunderclap and I am seared to nothing — mere bones falling into ash.

CHAPTER TWO

I am grateful to be home again, safe inside my own four walls, with blinds I can close and doors that lock. Behind my house there is a brook and a path that runs beside it, disappearing into the forest, stretching back as far as my land goes. I repaired the path myself the first summer after I bought the house, hacked at the underbrush, the alders and the goowiddy, because I like to work hard and feel myself sweat. It reminds me that I am his daughter as well as hers, that it is not only Bristow blood that steams in my veins, but Goulding blood as well.

I cannot abide anyone else using my path. The reason why I bought this house in the first place was to find somewhere that would enclose me, safe and stationary, like a fetus preserved in alcohol. I require blinds upon all the windows, blinds that can be immediately flattened hard against the glass, just in case someone happens upon my property or comes too close to the house. It is eccentric, and I realize this, but as a writer I must tailor certain aspects of my immediate environment to my requirements. I have often altered myself to suit the needs of others; now I intend to comfort myself first. I wonder if I have the courage. *You're so lazy as a cut dog,* she says inside my head, *dirty little scunner, I don't know what I'm going to do with you, you looks like something no one owns.* Her superior morality makes her able and fit to judge everyone around her, including and especially me. I wonder what makes

someone desire such all-consuming righteousness. I imagine even
the elect in Heaven get bored with it after a while. I would much
rather take a seat in Hell, close by the fireplace and plied with
cognac, a companion for the most notable of the heretics: F. Scott
Fitzgerald, Ernest Hemingway, drunk and clinging to each other;
William Burroughs, attended by giant cockroaches more intelligent
than himself; Henry Miller dancing past with Anaïs Nin, deserving
of Hell in her own right. Pragmatic as I am, I don't think I could
abide an eternity walled up with my mother and her kind.

When I check the path I discover several beer cans, chip
packets, a wad of gum stuck to the top of one of my fenceposts.
They have been here again, probably while I was at Elsinore:
occupying my property like vagabonds, swearing and spitting,
laughing at each other's vulgar jokes with barks and grunts. I
kneel on the mushy ground, feeling the November moisture
seeping through my slacks, and I collect their refuse as if each
item were some kind of artifact. Why do they do it? Immediately
my mind calls up the probability of vindictive purpose. Like
others of their age, they desire the annihilation of the adult world,
release from all its strictures. I remember myself that way: anxious
to be gone from childhood, eager for the careful transit of the
intellect and all the senses from the shell of myself to the new
creature I would become.

*Where's you going with that old garbage on your eyes? I suppose
you're going out with the rest of 'em, chasing the boys, is ye? Sure,
what fellow is going to have you? Look at yourself. Go in the bathroom and wipe that shite off your eyes. And put on something decent.
Going out in public with the like of that on — sure, I won't be able to
show me face over to the store no more. Don't you think more over
yourself than that?*

Debbie Bristow, a distant cousin, was having a birthday party.
I was fifteen, and even though my father didn't hold with
dancing, I wanted to go so badly I could taste it, a sweetish odour

in the back of my throat. Debbie was the prettiest girl in the school, and she always had nice clothes; when Debbie wore her black hair long and full, the rest of us did, too, and those whose hair was short resolved to grow it right away. When Debbie came to school in baggy jeans and an Aran sweater, with white socks and Chinese shoes, there was a flurry of excitement. On Monday morning, an army of young girls appeared in baggy jeans and Aran sweaters, or whatever approximation could be got up at short notice. We all mooned about her as if she were the earthly embodiment of style, and it is to her credit that she was gracious to the parade of imitators that trailed after her that year; she seemed to understand the responsibility of beauty. In typical style, she had invited everyone, even tiny little Anita Fifield with her chicken neck and her thick glasses. Because it was Debbie's party, there would be lovely things to eat and a carefully prepared non-alcoholic punch, served in tiny glass cups. The music would be tasteful and trendy, and everyone would arise in unison to dance, girls with girls, acutely conscious of our movements, not wanting to appear too eager or too precocious.

I had never been one for parties, knowing the state of my social skills. Whenever I managed to go to one of these things, I ended up feeling slightly ill-used, even though no one had offered me any insult. I compared myself to the other girls, weighed my attributes and achievements, and found myself wanting. It was a contest that I could not win, a race in which I could not hope for so much as a courtesy title; it was won by girls with mothers who sewed or knit, who belonged to the Ladies' Auxiliary at church. It was a social sport, it was not for someone like me, and I knew it.

I waited until I thought my mother was in a good mood, gauged my chances according to her unsteady emotions. I'd been a good girl, I told myself, I had not pestered or tormented her, nor had I begged or asked for anything. I believed that these statistics would achieve victory.

I found her lying on the bed in her room, the drapes drawn against the scourge of late-afternoon sun. She had a headache, she'd told me earlier, and her unconcerned, even dismissive manner gave me hope. Also, it was summer, and I believed that the gentleness of August inspired in her an attitude approaching kindness, although I had only seen this once or twice.

"Mother?" I pushed open the door and approached her bed as one comes to the altar, seeking both salvation and the scourge of penance. She lay in a pose of resignation, a damp washcloth on her forehead. "Mother?" I reached my hand out; her arm lay undefended on the eiderdown. Perhaps I might touch her flesh for an instant, and she would never notice.

"Get me a glass of water." Her eyelids flickered, her eyes rolled beneath them, bulbous with dreams. "Me head is pounding that much I feels like I can see the face of God."

I handed her the glass, waited while she drained it and set it on the nightstand. "Mother." I took a deep breath, decided it was best to spill it as quickly as I could. "Debbie's having a birthday party and I'm invited and all the other girls are going and I wanted to go, too." A pause, the indrawn breath of hope.

"Debbie *who?*" She placed the washcloth over her eyes, masking herself.

"Debbie Bristow."

"Eileen Murphy's girl?" Her lips moved, formed each word precisely. "She was Eileen Murphy before she married Dicky Bristow. My God, I knew Dicky Bristow when I was young, before I had you."

"So can I go?"

She peeled the cloth away, peered at me, her eyes as cold and blue as the naked underside of an iceberg. "Go where?"

I forced myself to swallow. "To Debbie's birthday party."

A wet slap, the washcloth settling back against her eyes. "No, and that's what you can't. That's all I wants — you going up there and making a holy show of yourself. Next thing Eileen Murphy'll be over to the shop yakking about how I sent you up to Debbie's party in something not fit to put on your back." She laughed. "Lord Jesus Christ, it's not like I could find anything for ye to wear, ye're that hard to fit."

I will not cry for her, I thought. *Not this time, not now, not ever again.* But even as I thought it, my eyes filled with tears. "Okay," I said, in a voice dragged from the abyss. "Thanks anyway."

I closed the door quietly behind me, my hand pressed hard against my mouth so that the involuntary noises would not escape within her hearing, prove her devastating power over me.

It was like the time I'd started examining my own breasts for lumps after a film the school nurse had shown our grade eleven health class: matronly women in flowered housedresses, smiling while they manipulated their breasts in concentrated, meditative silence. We were old enough not to laugh and giggle, but we didn't look at each other, either. After the film was over Darlene Mitchell — morbidly obese with huge feet and kinky orange hair — farted quietly and got up from her seat, pretending that she didn't care or that she hadn't done it, while blood distilled slowly into her pendulous cheeks. Nobody had the courage to laugh, but Doris Coady wrinkled her nose and muttered, "What a goddamn stink" as we all filed out into the hallway. Jeanette Myers hit Darlene with her shoulder as she and Angie Button swaggered by, and Jeanette shouted, "By the Jesus, gonna be feelin' me own tits the night." I laughed, glad that I was not the object of their ridicule, pleased that their enmity was directed towards someone else for once.

That night, after my bath, I closed myself into my room and tried to remember what the women in the film had done. I felt silly, touching my own breasts, pushing them around in that fashion — as if I had some kind of bizarre fascination with my own flesh, as if I would willingly fondle myself, as if I were not repulsed by every evidence of my mortal body. I knew that I was ugly; even if Mother had not felt the need to impress this knowledge upon me, I had the testimony of my own eyes.

How can I phrase it? My fingers happened upon something very like a lump, a ball of gristle. A peculiar sensation, when, in the pause between heartbeats you come face to face with your own mortality: *I will not live forever, after all.* I was frightened with that fear that strikes ice into your bones. "Mother?" I found her in the kitchen, playing cards around the table with Aunt Marion and Cyril Beach's wife Phyllis. "Mother?"

I had wandered into their midst wearing my housecoat, a flowery thing that Nanny Bristow had given me for Christmas some years before. It had grown too small for me, had crawled above my knees with the passage of the years — a quilted dress, rather like an oven mitt. "What in the name of God Almighty do you want?" She looked up from her cards, her lips pressed hard together like a seam or a wound.

"I needs to talk to ye." I held the housecoat shut around myself, aware of them gazing at me, at my stubbled legs, the white flesh of my naked feet.

"Sure, talk to me, then." She glanced at Cyril Beach's wife and laughed, and Aunt Marion joined in, *That's a good one, Mim.*

"It's something private," I said. I didn't want the rest of them to hear it, so I went into my bedroom, shut the door behind us.

"What in the name of the world is wrong with you?" Her eyes snapped at me. "I'm out there, trying to have a bit of relaxation while your father's out on the water, and you got to spoil it. You spoils everything. I can't have nothing with you around. I'm going to run away, now, and that's the god-blessed truth."

"I got a lump in me breast." I had to whisper it, gazing past her shoulder as I always did. "I was feeling my breasts for lumps and I found it."

"Mauling at yourself again." She pulled open the front of my housecoat, stared at my body. "Which one is it?"

I waited while she prodded me, her long nails driving into my flesh, her eyes flinching from me. "Nothing wrong with you," she finally said. "That's the inside of your nipple you feels, that's all."

I wanted to cling to her, as I would cling to a mother; I wanted us to weep in each other's arms like comrades. "Are you sure?" *Reassure me, love me, tell me that I'm not going to die.*

"Go way, for the love of God. Healthy girl like you. Sure, you'll live to be a hundred." I must have wept a little bit, relieved. "Stop snottin' and bawlin', now. Big baby, it's time you grew up."

I listened to her out in the kitchen a moment later. "In there tissin' and bawlin' like a little youngster. Thought she had a tumour" — chew-mor — "in her breast." Guffaws, women's laughter. "Sure, I'm full of tumours, meself. Now are you in for this hand, Phyllis, or what?"

It was nothing to her, an annoyance, it was me coming up from the basement at eight years old, I'd torn the side of my finger open and it was streaming blood. *Sure, what are ye showing that to me for? I don't care.*

I would find myself wishing her dead and then sicken in a great wallow of remorse because she was my mother, after all, and I should not damn her so easily and so out of hand.

I cup the rubbish they have left behind, hold the cast-offs to my bosom like the artifacts they are. I need to close myself inside where it is safe, escape the scourge of life as it torments me with tokens of itself.

I have an editor, like most authors, and every two weeks or so he telephones me, like people do when checking up on sick relatives, the elderly and invalids. His name is Liam, and he's tall and thin and Irish, with skin paler than mine and eyes of no colour I have ever seen before. He went to school in Armagh, and his father was a bus driver and his mother was a nurse. He has a sister, he told me once, who is married to an engineer in Ontario and who dotes upon their twin boys, Declan and Max. I ask Liam how they managed to choose names like Declan and Max, and he tells me that his sister wanted Irish names while her husband wanted something modern, and they compromised. It strikes me as the silliest thing I have ever heard, this ado about names. Why would people invest so much time and energy in such an enterprise? I have no idea why I was named *Stella Maris Goulding*, unless it was some sly joke on my mother's part. Stella Maris, Star of the Sea, Our Lady who guides the foundering ship to safety, the Mother comforting the dying sailor. I wonder what my naming means.

Liam is telling me something about the new book, the one I just finished and handed over to him. I find myself not really listening to what he's saying but instead following the cadence of his words, the rhythmic rise and fall of his accent. "Five thousand copies to start with . . . Stella?"

"I'm here." Liam always knows when I have been daydreaming.

"But not listening, that's for bloody well sure." But he isn't angry. Liam is never angry, at least not with me. It's as if he believes that I am some fragile vessel, apt to shatter. I enjoy the idea.

"I'm sorry. I haven't been sleeping well lately." A lie — I sleep as deeply as I ever did, like a death, a blink, a coma. I find myself wondering, as Liam speaks, how it would feel to sleep for weeks or months, to hibernate. Do bears dream dreams, see visions, when they lie like lead in their dens? What sorts of visions do they see? And do they hear the hushed and muffled sounds of winter, or are they deaf, blind, insensible? I think I might like to sleep like that, a sleep one pace or two removed from death itself.

"Five thousand copies, the first print run? The art department sent me up some slides the other day so we can help pick the image for the cover." He sounds amused, as if he might be standing next to me and studying my features as usual. "Do you want to get together, or should I put them in the mail?"

"No, put them in the mail." I can't allow anyone in here, not even Liam, whom I have known since I finished university and who has been my editor for what feels like forever. "I'll look them over on the weekend and tell you which ones I like. You can pick. You're better at that sort of thing than I am." This is true: Liam has an artist's eye and a feeling for the mystical. This is just as well, because the books I write are fervent, sometimes fevered explorations of those almost-monsters that live around the edges of consciousness: the Daone Sidhe, the Tuatha de Danaan, mermaids and sea monsters, ghosts and spirits, the Faeries and the Fhain, the Black Kelpie, Tam Lin the demon lover, the selkies. *Gone to get a selkie skin to wrap the baby bunting in.* Mother's voice: *don't go down by the water.* But there was nothing, only the nightly migration of local men carrying slop pails down to exorcise their contents in the ocean.

"There's some Elena Demova in there. Some new stuff." We have used the paintings of Elena Demova on every single one of my other books: there is a visceral, savage quality to her work that greatly appeals to me, a kind of Ginsberg "Howl" in two dimensions. For my first novel we used a painting called *You and the Stars*: a woman's face, fragmented, picked out against swirling stars. Liam likes her work as well, and I think he himself has visual inclinations. I wonder sometimes why he is a book editor, but he insists he likes the work.

"Are you all right?" he asks me before he rings off. Liam always asks me this.

"Perfectly fine." This is true insofar as most lies have a shade of truth to them; ever since Elsinore I have a disturbing idea that I am to be somehow invaded by my mother. In what fashion, I cannot say. I only know that her spectre is likely to stalk me when and where I least expect it.

I proffer some blandishments and Liam goes away, satisfied that I am not about to vanish. I am grateful to him because he is perhaps my only link to the real, practical world. I appreciate the buffer he provides, the way in which he goes beyond his role. At book launches (which terrify me) Liam pilots me about the room as if I were mounted on casters; he is especially adept at intercepting over-zealous postulants who rush at me, arms outstretched as if to tackle me. I remember how, at a literary dinner in the Newfoundland Hotel, Liam skilfully out-manoeuvred a three-hundred-pound female with eye-watering BO and a beard to rival Farley Mowat's. She had written a novel, she said, and she insisted that I read it, and then she threw her fleshy arms about me and pressed all the air out of my lungs as if she were squeezing a bellows. I am forever grateful to Liam, as I have never been grateful to any other man; unlike the others, he has a purpose that is, at least for me, clearly defined.

I keep a tray of houseplants by the kitchen window, small ones, the prickly cacti with their juicy stems reposing in an empty Lean Cuisine container, grouped together as if whispering. There is a fern, feather-finned and as mysterious as sea horses, sensitive to the slightest change of air pressure, attuned and turning always to and from the source of its discomfort. I have a Joseph's Coat, velvety and pink; I found a sea plant once between the rocks down on the beach at Elsinore, a Joseph's Coat, or near enough, food for water whelks and periwinkle.

We found things in the ocean, always. I remember being six or seven and digging about underneath stones compressed into the size and shape of manhole covers by the sea. Barnacles, miniature mountains encrusting these flat plates, crumbling into an ashy dust, old bones and ancient teeth; a tansy, sleek and thin, tube-like, darting in the shallow tidal pools like a demented, severed finger.

Its teeth, they said, could cut your hand off, but I could never understand how a thing so tiny could devour other beings whole.

My mother is only five feet tall but always felt much taller to me; I would bring her things, the dried and empty casings of some ocean animal or a certain type of seaweed, I don't remember which — we called them mermaid purses, and we would gather tiny stones to fill them with imagined bounty. The smell was somewhere between the coarse, abrasive scent of stone and the tangy prick of salt. At night, I would lie in bed and watch the moon traverse its wobbly course on my bedroom walls and smell the sea upon my fingers. I imagined I could hear a keening on the waves.

I saw a dolphin once, trapped by drifting pack ice and forced back into the curving basin of the harbour. Again and again it would dive and surface, and from where I stood on the shore I could hear the rasp of its salty breath, drawn in and out, see the steaming spume exhaled into the freezing air. I knew that once the ice closed in, it would be trapped beneath; unable to surface for air, it would die. I knew a kind of melancholy that I had never felt before. I could do nothing to rescue it. I was helpless, like my father in the springtime, bloodying himself upon the ice with seals, wading through the coiled nests of pelts, guts and blubber, smelling it inside his nose forever. Someone had to be a witness to the carnage. Mother would make flipper pie at Easter time, the hand-like appendages with their digits so very like fingers. Nanny Bristow said it was a sin to kill a selkie.

I feel, in the midst of this diatribe, that there should be some rhyme or reason to my memories, but there is none — at least none that I am able to supply. Something is rotting, away down deep in memory's bilges — something that smells like seawater, something that has the metallic taste of blood.

My father always called me Nancy-O. I remember, when I was a tiny child and he a fisherman, how he would come home, and I would meet him running, running down our lane, the cold wind lifting the hem of my little-girl dress, my arms outstretched. I don't remember this at all, but it is what they tell me, and over the years and with many tellings, it has achieved the flavour of a legend. Besides, it is a pretty story, and I am inclined to believe it for the simple reason that I require something pretty to remember about myself. He would catch me in his arms and say, "There's my Nancy-O" because that was his favourite song, "My Nancy-O." Nanny Bristow told me later that he'd had a sister who'd died of TB when she was five; her name was Nancy, and her hair was as red as the setting sun. It was the Irish in them, Nanny said. Everybody knew that Goulding was an Irish name.

I remember most of all the salty smell of his clothes, his sweater of rough-spun wool, and how his fingers had deep cuts in them, like furrows worn in wood. He'd sit beside the stove at night and break the waterpups that formed around his wrists, hissing at the pain but never crying out, muttering softly to his blisters, *Ye bastard ye hurt that time, didn't ye?* And he would rub Chase's Ointment into his skin and bind clean strips of flannel round his wrists, like the flannel strips that Nanny Bristow used for curlers in my hair.

I believe I loved him, but I can't be sure. I always thought of him as a man beyond any kind of reckoning, a man whose every feature, every attribute, was as clear and plain upon his face as daylight. He'd play games with me when he was home: "Button Button Who's Got the Button?" and "Cat's Cradle" and "Guess What Number I'm Thinking." He was always thinking of nine, but I would pretend otherwise and count as high as I could, careful to steer clear of nine so as not to guess too easily and hurt his feelings. I imagined him to be delicate, vulnerable and fragile, and I knew I had a duty not to break our pact by exposing him. He was illiterate and innumerate; he could write his name, laboriously and by concentrating very hard on the shape of each individual letter. It was something he had learned by sustained viewing, as one commits a landscape to memory. He was not a stupid man. He possessed acuity of vision. He was honest. He was a disappointment to my mother, who believed that by marrying him she would acquire something of potentially great value, like the acres of barren granite that yield up a nation's worth of minerals.

He kept his fishing premises across the road from our house, "the rooms," he called it, and I would go across and sit upon a buoy while he knitted up his nets, the long twine needle flashing through the diamond shapes that formed the mesh. Sometimes it would move almost too fast for my eye to follow, and the outline of both it and his hand would achieve a kind of blur, a rupture in the bubble that encased us. Then I would hear a humming, perhaps the sound of twine unspooling and marrying with the mesh, a shuttling of octaves between the imagined and the truly sensed, a sound like whale song.

He was seldom around when I was small. I don't blame him for this, he had to earn a living, he had to feed my mother and me, keep up the payments on the boat. Looking backwards now, I truly can't blame him for wanting to be elsewhere. I know how difficult it was to live with Mother; I would not have wished it on anyone, and certainly not on him. In the winter, he would be down in the rooms, with a wood stove made out of an old oil drum to keep the cold away, prevent his fingers from stiffening so he could no longer knit the twine. I would go and watch him, sit and ask him, *How come you does that, Father?* And when he tired of my incessant questions, he'd give me a quarter and tell me to go to the shop.

Here it is on the windowsill, shiny and round, a gleaming disk like the face of the moon, holding promise in its curves, a never-ending arc, a circle with no beginning and no end. Whenever I see a shiny quarter, I think of my father: I think of him getting up early to go fishing and stepping quietly into my room, laying something on my bureau with his blunt, thick fingers. I would awaken in the morning and find a half stick of Doublemint and on top of it, gleaming like an offering, a brand new quarter, all mine. Whenever

I see a shiny quarter I think of him, and holding this one now between my fingers, sensing the rub of its serrated edge, I think about the calluses on his hands, and I remember how he used to hold my squishy little fingers. Sometimes I'd find him down there in the rooms, standing by his stove, his twine needle flashing in the early dusk, and he'd be singing old hymns from his childhood in the Salvation Army: *My father is rich in houses and lands, He holdeth the wealth of the world in his hands.* He had a rich voice, rumbling out of his chest like Triton's laughter; he was a god to me.

Standing by the window and gazing out now into the November twilight, I am reminded of him with a pain that is as poignant and as bitter as a bone lodged in my throat. I look down at my hands, my fingers, and see him written there in flesh, in smaller scale. I have his hands, she always said. *You're just like your old man, sure.* I miss him, and I know that nothing I say or do will ever bring him back again. He was an integral sort of man, a man without whom the earth cannot comfortably rotate; it is unthinkable that I shall never see him again.

A quarter to go to the store . . . the nylon legs of my snowpants whisking together, marking every step with an insectile sound, which I would hum to — *hmm-hmm-hmm-hmm* — under my breath. I would watch the trails of vapour steaming out of my nostrils, and the snow underneath my feet would be hard and squeaky, holding the imprint of my winter boots. I can see her now with my inner vision; I can see her walking down the main road of Elsinore towards the grey wooden building in whose windows lights burn against the early night. Fifield's Store: a two-storey house with pretensions towards the mercantile and the green of Dust-Bane on the floor. The little girl, who reaches a mittened hand up to the door latch, the old tongue-and-groove door, the outdoors door, the bay. She can barely see over the counter, and the shop girl watches her with gimlet eyes, Alice Fifield's other daughter Lucy, Lucy who was in the car accident (*Her father was drinkin', he's nothing but an old drunk, sure*) and had to wear braces on her legs underneath her slacks. Lucy, with straight black hair cut across her forehead in a fringe, like pictures of schoolgirls in the old days: my mother standing next to Eva Bailey and squinting into the camera, her unruly hair escaping from the scarf that clamps it to her head. "Juicy Lucy" the boys call her, but never to her face, because everybody knows the Fifield women all have bad nerves — it's on account of Mr. Fifield's drinking. It is an open secret in Elsinore, and Hartley Tizzard swears, hand on the Bible, sir, that he seen Mr. Fifield in his black Chev, weaving back and forth across the yellow line, coming out of Elsinore one night. Drunk, he was. And him standing up in the United Church on Sunday then, and singing hymns with all the rest of them, after what he done to Lucy. Should be ashamed of himself. Got no right even showing his face in public, now, and that's the way it is.

How often condemnation is sounded in my mother's voice, how easily judgement trades upon the cadence of her speech. I turn the quarter in my fingers, thinking of my father, and I believe I know why he ran away to sea.

There was a story years ago about Aunt Val's husband Ivan, and how he had got aboard a schooner bound for Labrador and was never seen again. It was like the shipwreck of the *Rose*, some said: a schooner floating bottom-up, somewhere in the Straits, no survivors, nothing left except the flotsam. I always liked that word and imagined flotsam to have a kind of lightweight quality, like Styrofoam; when the tidal pools refilled at the tug of the moon, these floating particles would find their way inshore to clutter all the hollow places in the rocks. Aunt Val's husband went to sea in a two-masted schooner, and the boat was lost with all hands, lost without a trace. Someone said Aunt Val had driven him away, beating him about the ears with her ceaseless clamour; someone else insinuated that she had driven him insane, and he was even at this moment languishing in the Mental, gnawing at his bonds like a caged animal.

In certain northern islands off the coast of Scotland, women knit sweaters for their men. Each family has a pattern that is particular to it and bound up with its history; you would not think of using another family's pattern. Thus any man who is drowned can be identified by the pattern on his sweater when his body washes up on shore. They always wash ashore — it is impossible, I've found, to escape the flotsam when it wants to find you, when it wants to clutter up the hollow places in the dark.

I am gazing out the window, it is fully dark now, and I am turning this quarter in my fingers, feeling its rub against my skin.

I wonder if mermaids make streaming sweaters for their menfolk out of Irish moss. Seaweed upon the tide takes for itself the motion of the sea and mocks the whiplash flow of hair. A drowned body anchored underneath a shelf of stone might seem to be an angel or a mermaid.

CHAPTER THREE

The first night home, I dream of Elsinore again. I always go to bed early; otherwise I would stay awake all night, watching the news on television and listening to the radio: VOCM First News, every hour on the hour. I sometimes lie awake in the dark listening (through my opened windows, if it is summer) to the sound of the sea, muttering in the distance, or the pulse of a siren. There are ambulances and fire trucks; there are rescue squads that roam about at night enacting futile dramas, all of which are dutifully relayed to me: NTV Evening News, VOCM Eye in the Sky, CBC, CNN, the Internet. This is not a hobby; this is deadly serious. If I don't pay attention, something untoward might happen. I will awaken after it is over, too late for Armageddon. I will be left behind.

I cannot stay awake, however, and there's the rub: while my eyes are closed and I'm unconscious, the world goes on without me. Things happen in the night.

I dream of Elsinore: I am walking down the sloping road into the cove, through an avenue of thick-growing pines, tamarack and spruce. The hills of Elsinore are green, and the lilac trees that grow in our front yard are budding. I can smell them, and this is how I know I'm dreaming; no waking-world perception is this vivid. I am overwhelmed with scent, stupefied with fragrance.

Our house is the only house in Elsinore. Behind it, and beyond to where the rolling hills keep careful consort with the sea, there is nothing. There is nothing but the opalescent grey that is the sky, an uncertain shade like old men's beards or dandruff. My feet squeak on the road, even though my sneakers tread on gravel. I can only walk very slowly, as if my pace were predetermined by some condition of the dreaming.

The house is the same: the shallow entrance that opens almost directly into the living room, branching into the dining room that overlooks the stretch of land we call our own. I go to the window and look out, and I can see my mother pinning out the washing, down near the end of the yard. She is very tiny, and thus I intuit that she is far away. She tries to pin the same white object onto the line without success. Every time she is beaten back by the wind, and she grapples with the object, which I see is a man's white shirt, the arms and torso bellied out. I think it is my father's shirt, or maybe it is mine.

When I turn to make my way out of the house, I find that all the walls have changed their shape, and the corridor is gone. I am in the hallway, off which bedrooms lead, and there is the trapdoor in the floor that goes down to the basement, the basement where my mother lies dead. I do not think to question how she can be in two places at the same time. I know she is miraculous and capable of wonders. She can evade me easily.

I wake up in a sweat, my nightdress coiled around my waist like an inner tube, my heart throbbing hard enough to burst.

The phone is ringing. *Damn Liam*, I think, but it's not Liam. When I hold the receiver to my ear, an Englishman's voice berates me cheerfully. "What the bloody hell are you doing in bed, love?"

"It's . . ." I squint at the clock, unable to read sense into the shifting orange numbers. "It's very late, Sam." Sam is my pen pal, after a fashion; we correspond by e-mail every day, and sometimes he even sends me faxes. He lives in London, an actor in what people sometimes call costume dramas, and he often does some Shakespeare, he's told me. We've never met in person, but I know the way he looks because he's sent me photos. He's only ever seen my picture on the jacket of a book. I don't have the heart to tell him that no one looks like that, and certainly not me. I also cannot bring myself to confess the other truths to him — for example, the way I force myself to dress when I must go out, the costume drama that I myself enact. Even an actor might not understand. He'd think I was a freak, and I expect he's met his share of freaks. They say the Underground is filled with them.

I find my wristwatch on the bedside table: it's one in the morning. In London it is four-thirty, and what in God's name is Sam still doing up? I ask him, expecting some kind of witty retort, as usual.

But no. "I got a film role," he tells me. "In Canada, believe it or not." I imagine he means somewhere like British Columbia, somewhere far away from me.

I love Sam, insofar as it is possible for me to love anyone. He is handsome and kind and good; he loves life and he especially enjoys his work. As far as personality goes, he is exuberantly actorish, but I don't mind. He balances my morbid sense of the everlasting, and he is the only person, now that my father is gone, who can intuit for me some of the mystery of life. But I could never bear to be in physical proximity to him, close enough so he could reach out and touch my sleeve. If he did that, I would die: I would crumble into ashes like old bone; I would vanish into dust, become a handful of sand to slip between his fingers. I'm not good enough for him to touch, and I can't bear to have him near me. He is so sure of who he is and so attractive that he would be repelled by me, my loathsome physicality, and I don't believe I could bear that. No, it's safer this way, Sam thousands of miles away across an ocean and me here in Topsail. It's best that he not truly know me as I am.

"In Canada?" I force myself to sound pleased for him when in truth I'm terrified. I am also a little peeved that he has called so late and woken me up. "Where?"

"Rather near to your neck of the woods, as luck would have it."

Sam has one of the most beautiful voices I've ever heard; I could listen to him forever. I told him, after the very first time he'd ever phoned me, that they ought to pipe his voice into places such as dentists' offices to soothe people suffering through root canals, and he'd laughed and said I was absurd. "Nova Scotia, actually — place called Halifax."

My heart boomed in my throat, and my face felt prickly. "Halifax?"

"Yes. Perhaps we might be able to meet there, if you like. I've been looking at my trusty map, and it seems to me you're just a short hop away by airplane." There is a silence, and I know he is waiting for me to fill it. He has no idea that I could never answer such a pro-position with a simple yes.

"Yes," I say, surprising even myself. "Yes, that's right. Just a short hop."

"Or I could pop over there, you know." Like stepping onto a tram and being neatly deposited on my doorstep. "Spend the weekend, perhaps — in a hotel, of course." He is quick to correct himself; he will not go so far as to assume that some kind of intimacy exists. We have known each other for five years, if e-mails and periodic phone calls count. He is the only human being in the world besides Liam whom I allow close to me.

"Of course," I respond. And I add, "Congratulations on the film." I don't know what else to say. His world is so far removed from the narrow confines of my own that I cannot begin to relate to it, except in the most abstract and imaginary way. And yet I have seen all his films, many times over. Sometimes, late at night, when I am distracted by some thorny problem of character or plot, I will unearth his tapes and immerse myself in him. He cannot know how many times he has seen me safely to sleep. He would laugh if I told him.

"Well, better get to bed," he says. "Almost day." He's smiling, I can hear it in his voice; he is justifiably pleased with himself, and I am stabbed with guilt because I cannot be happier for him than I am.

"I'm proud of you," I whisper. Three thousand miles away, I know that he is smirking, sitting in his leather chair beside the window, twirling the phone cord around his index finger, his long legs dangling.

"Course you are," he says.

And then I am listening to nothing but the dial tone.

I get up and go through the house to the kitchen, find myself a carton of milk, and stand there, my backside pressed against the sink, and sip it slowly. I imagine him making the rounds of his house in Islington, locking all the doors and making sure the cat is in — I don't even know if he owns a cat. I imagine him going slowly up the stairs, pulling off his shirt as he goes and dropping it just inside the bedroom door —

I cannot allow myself images like these. It's too dangerous. I could so easily fall prey to his enormous appeal and lose myself. I cannot even be sure if I will meet him in Halifax, or if I said yes merely to placate him. If I hurt him, I would never forgive myself. He is pure, like bottled sunlight. He has never been broken.

I remember Phineas Tuck, Elsinore's town fool. Forty years old, he had the mind of a ten-year-old. Everybody was afraid of him, although children teased him mercilessly, hurling stones in summer and snowballs in winter. I was a little bit afraid of him myself, but mostly I felt bad that people picked on him. I lived under the illusion that he was an outcast like myself, unsure of his place in society and therefore unable to have any kind of active voice in the discourse; I pretended that we were comrades, that we shared an understanding. I secretly decided that the entire town had misjudged him: he wasn't merely an idiot, but something of a holy fool. If someone pressed discretely upon the hidden latch of his soul, prophecies would issue forth.

I remember a midwinter visit — it seemed always to be

wintertime in Elsinore — to Aunt Frieda Tuck's house, when I was ten. My mother had sent me with a two-dollar bill folded up inside my mitten to get eggs from Aunt Frieda because she was one of the few women left in Elsinore who raised hens. Aunt Frieda's eggs were brown, huge and sometimes still warm from the hens.

I sat for what seemed like hours in my winter coat and snow-pants, sweating next to the stove while my rubber boots dripped onto Aunt Frieda's much-abused green canvas floor. She brought me a glass of Purity syrup and a slice of cake, left over from Christmas and as hard as a slice of brick. I remember gnawing at it resolutely with my front teeth like a rat, trying to break through the crust to the sweetness that, I suspected, lurked beneath. It was an exercise in futility: the cake was as unyielding as concrete.

Aunt Frieda went off into the darkness at the back of the house. Built before the war, it was a ramshackle wooden affair, as such dwellings often are, with an Enterprise wood-and-oil stove in the kitchen. Several pairs of women's knickers were strung on a line over the sink and had stiffened in the still, hot air.

Phineas was standing on the other side of the stove making jerking motions with one hand, as if pulling on a cow's teat. He wasn't looking at anything in particular, but I imagined he was casting some sort of spell on me, something heinous and primeval, dredged up from secret tomes. I forced myself to look away, rested my gaze upon the sagging, turquoise-painted Ten Test walls, bowed out like the sails of a schooner.

"Phinny, stop dat, now. We got company, luh." Aunt Frieda's dirty pancake slippers shuffled forwards out of the darkness; Phinny was herded off into the living room. I imagined him still doing it in there — whatever it was that he'd been doing. "You take them eggs on home to your mother now, my love." Aunt Frieda passed the carton to me, and I relinquished the two-dollar bill. I had secretly hoped she'd forget to ask for the money, and I could keep it. I had envisioned all the ways in which I might spend such bounty — Spiderman comics, bubble gum, or a couple of those hard rubber Hi Bounce balls with the sparkles inside.

As I was leaving, Phineas appeared again, creeping around the archway, holding something in his hand: a wiggly, flesh-coloured worm, sticking out of his pants and peering at me with its single blind eye. "I got a snake," he said. His voice was husky, like a man's voice, and he had hair growing on his chin. I realized how wrong I'd been in supposing him to be somehow holy, a misguided outcast. He was an idiot like all the other idiots, a retard holding his bird and showing it to me as if it was some kind of big deal.

I am standing in the kitchen, sipping milk out of the carton, and my bare feet are cold on the tiled floor. It's two a.m., and I have stood here for an hour, dreaming the dreams of the past. It's five-thirty in London, and I imagine Sam lying fast asleep, naked and alone. I wonder if I whispered to him, down the peaceful conduit of dreams, would he hear me? And what would I say to him? *I love you.*

He is as elusive as the dreams I often have of whales stranded in the bay, whales beaching themselves upon the pebbly sand of Elsinore. Orcas, black and white, so perfect and so elemental as to seem a necessary portion of the landscape. Yet, for all that, I cannot ever remember seeing orcas anywhere near Elsinore, and none have ever beached there. Sometimes in early summer there are humpbacks, sliding past the ragged coastline of the island, silent and remote, pothead whales and basking sharks, the great wise eyes of a seal. I hear whale song in the dream, or perhaps it is a kind of keening. I cannot be sure, because even as dreams go it is ephemeral, frangible. As soon as I surface into anything like wakefulness, I try to grasp some shred of meaning, but always it eludes me. The only thing I ever remember is that there was whale song. Perhaps I sang it, too.

I go back through the house, turning off the lights, thinking of Sam at home in London, sleeping in his bed with the turgid flux and hum of traffic outside his window. In my imagination, I am perfect, a woman without flaw and not the shadowed mask of imperfections with which I choose to clothe myself. That perfect woman could slip into his bed beside him, and he would turn and take her in his arms, and this would be as natural to her as drawing her next breath.

I close myself into my bed as if I am sealing myself into an envelope, a last will and testament that must not be opened until the proper time. It is appropriate that I cloister myself like this. If I allowed myself to indulge in life, I would lose all that I have cultivated. I might become something. I might become somebody else.

CHAPTER FOUR

There is an old, abandoned lighthouse back home in Elsinore. I return there after Remembrance Day, braving the sudden cold of mid-November and the possibility of storms to oversee the placement of my father's headstone.

I find my mother entertaining Uncle Joss, sitting at the kitchen table next to the window. A pile of discarded teabags rises amid the detritus of cracked lobster shells, and Mother and Joss sit at intimate right angles to each other, sucking sweet tidbits of precious meat from inside the skinny legs. They haven't heard me drive up the lane, and I come upon them quietly, easing the kitchen door on its hinges, lifting it and carrying it backwards as if I were striking my colours in the presence of a conqueror.

Mother has dyed her hair — I notice this before anything — dark red, gleaming like old blood. Her fingernails, too, are painted in a shade not dissimilar to her hair. She has recently applied red lip-stick but has since eaten it away with food and laughter. I am surprised that I am able to despise her. It seems just yesterday that my father was put into the ground.

I haven't told her I was coming; I undertook the trip on my own initiative. All my mother had was what he'd left to her: the house, her wedding rings, the car she didn't know how to drive because it was a standard shift. I had ordered the very best stone from Muir's, had paid for it with my own money. I could not trust that it would be laid the way I wanted it, and I feared that if I did not oversee this very important duty, it would never be done properly.

"Where'd you come from?" As if she doesn't know, as if she thinks I have sprung from the ground like water.

"I got the headstone paid for," I tell her. "I came out to see if they put it up properly." I want to ask her if she's seen it, but I dare not. I want to believe in her essential goodness, even in the face of everything, and a word from her, some denigrating remark, would shatter my illusions. My mother and I have always been a bad fit, or probably it only seems that way because I have so often been forced to beg for whatever scraps of love she might drop along the way.

"Hello, Stella." Uncle Joss glances up at me, his lips flecked with lobster flesh. He eats the way seals feed, voraciously and all at once, and I imagine him cracking lobster shells between his teeth like nuts, crashing through the carapace as if through a thin layer of ice. "In from St. John's, are ye?" It is the stupidest question I have ever heard; I decide to ignore him.

"I'm going up to the graveyard," I tell my mother. She is occupied with the teakettle, pouring water in a hissing stream. She turns halfway around, fixes me in a speculative gaze the way some people might examine a strange insect. It is the Look, the Evil Eye, the gorgon's stare that can turn me into a block of stone.

"Sure, I don't care what ye does," she says, laughing without humour. "What're ye tellin' me for?" She elbows past me with the tea, clears a place for it amongst the shattered lobster shells. I wonder where she has got lobster in November. "Go on up there, if ye wants to. I don't give a jesus what you does. None of my business."

I am galvanized by her as always. It doesn't matter how I grow up or how I strive to separate myself from her, she will always hold dominion over me. I think of an incident in a shopping mall in town, an incident burned into memory by amused relations, who lose no opportunity to recount it. My mother has told the story time and time again, sitting around the card table with her friends, laughing over a hand of twenty-one, embroidering it and colouring the edges to suit her purposes. She uses it as she uses every story, to magnify herself, to cast aspersions on my version of the tale, as if my memory were faulty or I had rearranged the segments to make her look bad. I sometimes wonder if this is so — what if I were truly trying to cast her in a bad light and didn't even realize it? The idea makes me feel guilty.

The story is this: I am in a shopping mall with my mother. I am four years old, and I have been misbehaving constantly. My mother drags me behind a display of bath towels to give me what she always called "a hammering," but I escape her, elude her grasp, slip away from her and run down the wide centre aisle of the store, screaming as I go: *Don't hit me, Mummy, don't kill me.* I am finally apprehended by two nuns, who hide me behind their skirts when my mother comes charging down the aisle, mortified and trying hard to conceal it. There follow the usual facile explanations: *She's got some imagination. She makes up stories. Just like her father. Oh no, I'd never lay a hand on her. She's my darling, aren't you? Give Mummy a kiss. Give Mummy a hug.*

Being dragged out into the parking lot, her fingers clamped around my wrist, my arm stretched to its limit, the toes of my Winnie the Pooh sneakers being scuffed against the asphalt, and then the car - scrambling into the back seat, rolling over, trying to escape her hand as it rose and fell, her palm slamming into my flesh wherever she could reach: *Don't you* ever *say the like of that* again *or so* help *me God, I'll* kill *you.*

I crouched into a corner of the car's musty interior and screamed at her until I was hoarse: *I hate you. I hate your guts. I'm going to live with Nanny.* I pressed my feet against the back of her seat and kicked it as she drove, frustrated that I couldn't exert more pressure. I wanted to push her through the windshield.

I feel ashamed, realizing now what I had thought then. Halfway home, I hung over the back seat: *I loves you, Mummy. I'm sorry, Mummy. I loves you.* I tried to make her speak to me, but she wouldn't, only kept her gaze on the road, her hands white-knuckled on the steering wheel. I begged her to look at me, tried to turn her face to mine so I could see her eyes, patted her arm with my little childish hand and pleaded with her. *I loves you, Mummy. Mummy, I'm sorry, I'm so sorry.*

Her lips were set in a particular expression. I thought I had upset her, hurt her with my words.

I know now that she was smiling.

The road to the graveyard is one I know so very well, as if I had traversed it a thousand times, even though I haven't. It's just that it's so exquisitely engraved in my memory from the day of my father's funeral. Five hundred years from now, I will remember every detail as if it were passing again before my eyes.

Of course it's cold, as Elsinore is always cold; every memory I have of it includes the all-pervasive, deadening chill that seeps into every pore, that hardens the bones to the consistency of glass.

The narrow, gravelled road is hemmed in on either side by the clacking deadnesses of alders, scrubby spruce and juniper. I have walked this road before, sometimes alone and sometimes with my mother, during a period when we had struck a kind of truce, an uneasy peace. During the long evenings of summer, we would leave the house and, cardigans draped about our shoulders, stroll slowly about the perimeter of Elsinore. If I were very quiet and very well-behaved, she would sometimes deign to talk to me of her own childhood, before she had been so cruelly disappointed by her life and mine. When she spoke, I ceased to exist for her.

I never walk the roads of Elsinore alone; I am always walking with my mother. In my imagination, I am what she has always wanted me to be, I am perfect for her, and we are friends. In this version my mother loves me. If she knew how much I loved her in return, she would be astonished. I love her so much my chest hurts when I think of it. I love her so much that whatever lies she chooses to believe feel like truth to me.

I open the small wire gate and let myself into the graveyard. Set back from the gravelled road and overgrown with wild rose and alder, it gives the impression of great age, and the headstones appear to sink into the ground. It seems to hold the bones of Elsinore's ancient luminaries. I know the truth: it holds nothing but dust.

My father is buried in the far corner with all the other Gould-ings in their mesmerized repose. He lies next to his dead sister Nancy, who should have drowned or floated out to sea but died of TB instead when she was five. The image of Nancy floating in the sea is a romantic one, even though I know that drowned people bloat horribly, their skin bleached an unnatural white by the ocean's corrosive brine. Her granite headstone bears the carved face of an eyeless angel, the wings sprouting from the sides of the head like exaggerated ears or the amputated flippers of a seal. I am reminded of stories that Liam has told me about victims of the Famine and graves lined up in any piece of fallow ground found fit to hold them.

I realize I am on my knees in the cold pre-darkness, kneeling here and fingering the headstone of a girl who is my aunt — who would have been my aunt but is not because she was not present in the world when I was born. What sorts of gifts would she have cast about my cradle, appearing in the doorway with a distaff in her hand, My Nancy-O?

My father lies submerged in his own hole in the ground. I see that they have delivered the headstone and that it is properly set in concrete, just as I requested. There is no lengthy inscription, just his name and the dates, but I have asked for and they have delivered a beautiful carving of a two-masted schooner.

I had forgotten how early it gets dark; I am barely able to see the latch of the little wire gate, but I must take care to fasten it so the dead do not escape. And then I am walking down the dusty little road again, and the few streetlights in Elsinore are coming on one by one.

There is an old, abandoned lighthouse in Elsinore, and like most structures of its type, it is difficult to reach. First there is the journey out of Elsinore itself, around the point of land that juts out into the icy North Atlantic, across the front steps of the United Church, and from there to the narrow path that skirts the water's edge. By staying in the very centre of the path and following it through the keening marshes and over the top of Fifield's Hill, you eventually come to a shallow depression in the ground, rather like a fairy ring, and in the centre of this sits the lighthouse.

Once a man lived in it and kept the light, earned his living by polishing the great lenses and the huge reflecting mirrors, but now there is no one. The ground for several yards around is speckled with flakes and shards of red paint, the remnants of an ill-advised make-work project a summer or two ago. The irregular stone walls of the building shed curls of paint all on their own, and I can't help thinking that the wind and the sea will scrape it clean if left to their own devices. Everything erodes, given sufficient time, sufficient latitude to change.

I used to come here as a child, after school or on sleepy summer Sundays, sit on the edge of land closest to the ocean and imagine that I heard whale song. I would recall the old stories that Nanny Bristow used to tell me — of selkies shedding their animal skins to take on human form, of sailors drowning in the depths of the sea, of ghostly ships drifting forever on the eternal, faceless ocean. I wondered how one went about becoming a selkie, or if one was born to it or damned to it. *Whose idea were you, anyway?* my mother used to ask me.

I am surprised to find the door unlocked, and I pull it open and go in, never pausing to question my right to be here. My steps sound hollow on the concrete floor. Rising in an awesome spiral above me is the lighthouse's great iron staircase, as perfectly symmetrical as a conch shell.

"Hello?" I speak merely to hear my voice captured by this hollow tube; I am Alice, calling down the rabbit hole. "Is there anyone here?" I feel deliciously myself, whatever that is.

I make a circuit around the inside of the building, careful to go clockwise so as not to break the magic I am making. When I have walked the circumference three times without ceasing, I sit down in the centre of the floor, my hands clasped around my knees. I think I am waiting for something, but I can't be sure.

I have no idea of time as it whistles past me, or even that it is passing at all. I feel like I do at home when I have stepped into my study, lit a candle or a stick of incense, lain down on the floor and, staring into the flame, moved freely in whatever other realms there are. I feel the same sense of floating, of detachment from my mortal skin, of rising some small distance above the crown of my own head and hovering there, existing in that hum, that everlasting.

Someone is singing, a woman or a young girl; it sounds like stones crooning fables to the stars. Words form inside the cavern of my mouth but I lack the skill to shape them properly. All I know is that this is what I have always felt here in this place, and it is only mine and no one else's. My mother cannot have this.

The girl is young, barefoot and dressed in something that I have never been able to see properly: a shift of some kind, or a dress, or a clever collection of rags like a Cornish well-dressing. The red hair always seems to make perfect sense to me, at least while this is happening. *My Nancy-O, My Nancy-O.* Her face, what I can see of it, is dead white, as white as bone, and instead of eyes she has holes, black and charred about the edges as if burned by sulphur or the ocean. Why am I not afraid of her, why have I never been afraid of her?

No matter how often I see her — and I have seen her many times — she is essentially the same: bare-legged, wretched, abandoned like driftwood. I believe her ragged clothes are always streaming water. I can't imagine what she might be singing. I am not arrogant enough to think she might be singing to me.

She disappears up the spiral stairs, and this time I follow her, even though she is only a scrap of white, disappearing faster than I can move. At the very top I catch her, but only for an instant; her mouth moves, shaping words which sound to me like my mother's plaint that night on the phone, the night my father died. *The old man's gone. Won't be back no more, no.*

She leaps into where the light would be, and I am all alone again. I pace back down the stairs, walk the widdershins to break the circle I have made, and let myself out into the night.

I don't know where in the name of the world she went to — bolted out of here like someone said something to her. Sure, I don't know what's wrong with her to begin with, although I think she was always a bit soft in the head. Like her father's crowd, like Marion and them. Of course, Marion and the other one, that Eleanor, they always thought they were better than me. Oh, Marion would pretend, be right nice in front of my face, but I daresay her tongue was going when her and Eleanor was still living at the old house.

I don't know why in the name of God Stella had to come traipsing out here for. She can't leave well enough alone — she could never leave anything alone. Even when she was a youngster, she had to be picking and poking at stuff. I remember once when she was small, when Jack was home from the fish, and we were, you know, staying in bed kind of late one morning. Stella would always be up early, frigging around with stuff in the kitchen, even when she was right small. Trying to make stuff out of this little cookbook my mother got for her off the back of the Carnation milk tin — I don't know what she was thinking about, I honest to God don't. Stella ruined a dozen eggs one morning trying to make breakfast. The whole house stunk of burned eggs, and if you ever smelled it, you knows how hard it is to get that out of the house. You'd think someone had been burning turr feathers in the stove, it stunk that bad.

Me and Jack were trying to stay abed late that morning. Stella is out there in the kitchen, frigging around, clanking pots and pans, and I'm getting right pissed off with it. I even said to Jack, "So help me God, I'm going to kill that youngster before it lives to grow up." I think she was about seven or eight — no more than seven.

Anyway, here she comes in the bedroom, didn't even bother knocking on the door, and if I told her that once, I told it to her a hundred jesus times, *Knock on the bloody door.* But she don't hear nothing, see, it don't stay in her head no time. She's after falling down that many times as a youngster and banging her head, never mind the time Rita Bugden ran her over with the car, whatever brains she got are flat as pancakes. Didn't think no more of it than fly in the air, just come on in the bedroom, and Jesus Murphy if she didn't have something slopped on the plates, more eggs, half cooked and half raw, with the whites all watery, enough to turn your guts. I nearly threw up just looking at it.

Of course, here's Jack trying to get a bit off — you knows what the men are like, that's all they thinks about — and there's Stella standing in the doorway with all that frigging rubbish on the tray and cups of watery tea poured up. "I brought yer some breakfast," she says then, the little bugger, in this wheedly little voice that makes me want to smack the mouth off of her.

Here was Jack on top of me, getting ready to do his business, and there's Stella. Well Lord Christ, didn't I get mad. I shouted at her, and God knows, I hates to be shouting at youngsters, but Stella's that stunned, the only way she understands anything is if you bawls at her. She took the tray right quick and went on out again, her lip pouting out like she was going to bawl. "Don't you bawl," I told her. "Don't you dare bawl. I'm not having it."

When I went looking for her then I couldn't find her. God only knew where she went to, she was always a one for hiding in closets, used to crawl in on top of the old coats at my mother's house, in picking among the old rubbish she keeps, trying on old hats. She was always soft in the head, that youngster. I never knew what in the name of God she was up to, from daylight to dark. I couldn't find her, and God forgive me if I didn't go hiking up and down the whole bloody house, scoating me guts out, shouting and bawling for her. Here she was in the hall closet, then, sitting on top of the clean sheets. Always hiding in the closet like a lunatic. And the sloppy old eggs, then, hove down into the sink like a bucket of snots. Oh, didn't that burn me up. You'd think we had money to throw around.

I never wanted Stella — God forgive me, it's the truth, and I can't make out no other way. I never wanted her. She was something that come up, something there like a wart or a pimple. Honest to Jesus, she was like something I couldn't get rid of, and God knows, I tried, I might as well be truthful about it. I took that many hot baths, and I'd come out as red as a lobster, all queer in the head, like I was going to faint away. Eva told me that if you put an aspirin into a bottle of Coke and shook it up and then drank it, you'd get your period, and I remembered that. I took a few cents I had hid away in the pocket of my old school uniform, and I went out to the shop. I wasn't showing or anything — I never even told my mother, sure, not right then. I went out to the shop and got a bottle of Coke and did what Eva said, but it only made me stomach-sick. Didn't do no good after all. Of course, none of it do. You always thinks it will, but it never do. None of that works. I tried throwing myself off the bed, but my mother got pissed off with me thumping on the floor and told me to give it up or she was going to swipe the hunger off me.

I couldn't get Stella to go away. I used to try and push in on my stomach to try and force it out of me. I didn't know very much. We didn't have a school nurse in them days. You had to figure things out for yourself, and my mother never told me anything, she was too embarrassed, even if she was a nurse. Eva and I got hold of a book one time with pictures in it, and we used to have this camp up in the woods made out of boughs, and we'd go in there and have a tin of drink between us and talk about boys — what they had, and that, and how you got babies.

I could never get rid of Stella. I only did what I did so Jack would have to marry me. I wanted to get away from my mother.

She was never a proper mother to me, you know. I don't mind telling you, and that's the truth. Even after she come home from the San, I felt like I was a stranger in me own house, like she didn't want me there. While she was gone, I had me own way of doing things, like cutting up the vegetables for supper and cleaning up the house, and she used to get right dirty with me for doing it my own way and not her way. She come into the kitchen one time when I was waxing the floor, putting the wax on first with the floor polisher we had, and making sure I had the floor all covered. I used to go in the corners with a piece of rag to make sure I got wax on them tiles in there, and in behind the stove. She come into the kitchen on her canes and stood there looking at me like I had ten heads, and then she said, "What're ye doing it that way for? That's not the right way." And shouting and bawling at me that I had the floor ruined. I felt so foolish I could have died. She come over to me then and grabbed me by the arm and dug her nails so hard so the blood almost come. "You're some frigging lazy," she said, "You're as lazy as a cut dog." I felt like two cents.

I remember one Christmas, me and Father trying to put up a few decorations, and putting the best face on it, even though it was hard because we had no mother at home with us. That was when she was in the San. I feels sick to me stomach even thinking about it now, I know it wasn't her fault, but I'll never forget it as long as I lives. I don't know if it was better when she was gone or better when she was home. Perhaps it was just as bad either way. That's what I told Stella once. Only I said it to her when she was asleep, and I don't think she heard me. I don't suppose she heard me. No. She was asleep.

Sometimes when you makes a mistake you can go back and fix it up, erase what you done wrong, like in your copy book at school, where you used to practice your letters when you was learning how to write. Sometimes you makes a mistake, though, and it's there for good, and you always got to be looking at it, it's right there in front of your face and you can't get away from it. I feels that sick and tired sometimes — I was always sick and tired. I should have listened to my mother and put Stella up for adoption, or went in St. John's and give her to the nuns.

She come up to me once when she was right small, she heard some of the youngsters talking, you know, the way youngsters does. She said, "Mummy, was I a mistake?" And I was doing something, ironing clothes or something, and I told her to go on out of it. "I don't know where you hears the likes of that to," I said. "Old foolishness going through your mind all the time."

She kept it up, though, she was that bull-headed, she wouldn't give it up. "Mummy, was I a mistake? Because Karen Parsons said that Anita Fifield said I was a mistake and you never meant to have me." And she stood there with her finger stuck in her mouth, biting at the skin like she always done. I don't know where she got that habit to, and you knows how dirty the paws are on youngsters.

"Take yer fingers out of yer mouth and go wash yer dirty paws. You makes me sick to look at you. I put clean clothes on you the smornin, and you're that filthy now you looks like no one owns ye."

"How come Karen said that?" Looking at me and waiting for

me to say something, and then poking at the iron when I stood it up on the board. I knew frigging well she was going to get burned, and the next thing you know, there's this jesus big blister on her thumb and she's screeching like the bloody hounds of Hell. I slammed the iron down and grabbed her by the hair of the head, so help me God, I was that mad I could of killed her. "What did I tell you? What did I tell you?"

"I don't know." Screeching and bawling, you'd think I was killing her. Makes me sick to think about it, the way she used to get on, you know. If anyone went by the house and heard it, they'd have me over to the RCMP, now, and that's the truth. I'd be up on charges. Of course, you're not allowed to lay a hand on 'em anymore, youngsters. You can't touch 'em because that's child abuse. Go way, for God's sake. Yes, I used to get a bit rough with Stella when she was small, but sure, it was no more than what my own mother did to me. It never done me no harm.

I feels stomach-sick when I thinks about it: Jack gone to the fish all the time and me stuck in the house with that frigging youngster. It's no wonder I'm the way I am, it's no wonder I got bad nerves. Sure, even nowadays I got to be going over to Dr. Stein up to the clinic to get something. If it wasn't for Joss, I'd be worse off than I am.

"I told you that you was going to get burned. How many times have I told you not to touch the jesus iron?" I smacked her across the mouth — not hard, I never hit her hard — to try and get her to understand. "You don't listen to a blessed thing I tells ye, I might as well stand on me frigging head and whistle Dixie. There's never no peace in this jesus house with you going on the way you are. Go way, for the love of Christ, ye makes me sick to look at ye."

"Karen said I was a mistake." Snivelling and tissing, and oh God, don't that make me mad. I can haul the eyeballs out of her when she does that.

"You're not a mistake." I told her. "I wouldn't be that frigging lucky. You're nothing but a curse to try me, that's all you are. Bloody good-for-nothing youngster." And I opened the door and booted her on down over the landing. It was the only bit of peace I had all day.

I felt bad after, though, so I got a few biscuits out of the jar and went out with 'em, but she was gone off somewhere. She was always off somewhere by herself, and God only knows what she got up to — down by the beach, picking around under the rocks, hooking up stuff on the end of a stick, catching a fish and cutting the guts out of him. You knows what cruel little buggers youngsters are. She used to get sculpins down under the rocks by Bax's stage and poke the eyes out of 'em with a darning needle and then put the poor buggers back in the water again. I thinks she was possessed, myself. And then she wondered why the other youngsters used to pick on her. Jesus Christ, sure, no wonder. The child was a freak of nature.

No, my darling, you weren't a mistake. You were deliberate. You're as deliberate as they comes.

CHAPTER FIVE

As much as I despise being back in Elsinore, there is a certain nostalgic quality about waking up in the bedroom I'd slept in as a child. The bed is still where it always was, underneath the window that faces the road, the closet still has no door, and there is no mirror in this room — there never was. Why does memory compel me to regard this place as the only haven I have ever known? This is false: if haven exists, then it exists at Topsail, in the fortress I have built there for myself, impregnable to anyone.

It is very early in the morning and barely light: cold November with its slow dawn, the chill that takes forever to fade even after the fire has been lit. I cannot imagine being here a hundred years ago, when everything depended on one's own ability to transcend nature. Cold is still cold, however, and Elsinore is always cold. This house is cold, like old bones laid in the ground. My mother is still asleep.

I take the blanket from my bed and wrap it round my shoulders, sit on the edge of the bed and gaze out the window at the quiet. A thin coating of snow fell sometime in the night, and under the ministrations of the visiting moon this implausible outport of my childhood is transformed into something nearly mystical. I remember the girl at the lighthouse, and I wonder: where does she go when darkness fades, when the edges of the night are pared thin so as to allow the bulge of daylight. Perhaps the great light itself is her repository, and perhaps she lives there, like the ghosts in Scottish tales who exist inside a candle. I wonder what she is made of.

I dreamed about Sam last night; I have never dreamed of him before. I can't remember the particulars of the dream, only that he was there, and I was standing on a staircase speaking to him. He was sad, and I thought perhaps it was because of what I was saying, but I couldn't be sure. I remember in the dream I turned and walked away from him, and this somehow made him sad.

It's ten-thirty in the morning in London, where he is.

I find my clothes and go out into the kitchen, spend several fruitless minutes trying to light the stove, but it resists all my attempts. I am waiting for the electric kettle to boil when my mother appears, wrapped in her housecoat, the same old paisley one she always wears.

I am stunned into silence, realizing how old she looks, how old she has become. She cannot be more than fifty-five, but to me she seems infinitely ancient. Even the dyed hair, the painted fingernails cannot disguise the lines of resignation in her face, the crepey skin underneath her eyes and around her neck. This is how I will be in twenty years: shrivelled, desiccated like a shed skin, a pelt left upon the beach.

She ignores me as well, goes to the sink and hawks and spits into it, runs the water to flush whatever she has ejected, then picks up the kettle and shakes it at the end of its cord. I am still entranced by her movements, but now I see the slope of her shoulders, the upper back already beginning to round into a dowager's hump. She draws her upper body forward, a gesture of self-preservation; I have seen myself reflected unexpectedly in the windows of shops and know that I, too, exist in this truncated fetal crouch. Even disowned by her as I am — as I have always been — I carry some residue of her with me, something retained from my sojourn in her womb.

When she finally speaks, it is not to me and not to anybody. "I don't know what I done with the teabags. I had some yesterday." I remember that this was always a habit of hers, to talk even when there was nothing to say, even if there was no one but herself to hear. She is compelled to fill the air with noises of her own, she cannot endure the silence. She will not permit reading in her presence because the necessary silence is somehow an affront to her. Every moment, every aery space, must be filled with sound or else the vacuum will crush her.

"They're on the table, Mother. You left them on the table yesterday." I pick up the blue box and convey it to her at the end of my arm: the supplicant with the offering, unsure if the sacrifice will be acceptable or not.

Somewhere in the middle of this action, the door of my mother's bedroom opens. Like two people whose bodies are connected by a string, we both turn at the same time, but slowly. Uncle Joss is coming out of my mother's bedroom, wearing a pair of green work pants and a white singlet with a rip under the arm. His jowls are unshaven, sagging on either side of his neck; the hair on his chest is grey. I notice all these features with the meticulous sense of detail common to such situations. If called upon to testify, I am certain that I could provide a reasonable description. Yes, I know I could.

My mother, predictably, speaks first. "You want aigs fer yer breakfast or what?" I assume she is speaking to him, since she has never requested a menu of me. I feel as though I am trapped in a disastrous farce. *Bless my soul*, I find myself murmuring, over and over like an incantation or a mantra: *Bless my soul*. This is not something I am in the habit of saying. I have never uttered it before. I fancy I am possessed by some dead relative, that my body has been temporarily occupied by the vanished spirit of an ancestor.

I am moving even before I realize what has just occurred. I am moving towards the back hallway where my mother keeps the phone, and I am moving in that attenuated fashion typical of catatonics. I cannot find my bag with all my things in it, but I know the telephone number off by heart, I could recite it in my sleep. I watch my fingers stabbing out the sequence, listen to the strange double rings and hold my breath until I hear his voice: "Hello?"

I cannot speak; my body feels weightless, as if I have been running for a long time and am only now coming to rest. I try to think of how I will frame the sentiment. Are there any words for this?

"Hello?" he says again, his voice hazy with sleep, and then, "Is anybody there?"

"Sam." I feel as though I am choking.

"Stella? Stella, is that you?" I hear him arranging himself, and I know he's still in bed, that I've woken him. "What is it? What's wrong?"

I am crouching on the floor with the phone cradled against my ear, just so I can hear his blessed voice, and I am pouring it all out for him, pouring it all out and wondering why I don't feel foolish. I know I have to tell someone what I have just witnessed or it will double back upon itself, expand into the hollow places in my skull and crush me. Over and over again I see it, as if it were a movie projected onto the backs of my eyeballs: my mother shaking the kettle, Uncle Joss with the rip underneath the arm, *do you want aigs.*

"You mean they're having — having an affair?" Sam's voice is as clear as if he were in the next room, and just as disbelieving. "But your father is . . . I mean, he's not . . ." He trails off, unsure how far the boundaries of conventionality, of manners, will extend in this case.

I thank him for listening to me. I tell him that I hope he can go back to sleep, and then I ring off. I feel as if I will never sleep again, but I don't mind. I know that if I slept, I would dream of my father, be visited by his ghost, and I don't want that. To even contemplate it invites madness, and I cannot allow myself to go there.

While my mother and Joss are eating, I go into the pantry that is just off the back porch. This is the place where my mother keeps tins of Carnation milk and cardboard cartons of eggs, sacks of flour and dried white beans. I find an unopened bottle of Purity syrup — some indeterminate flavour, red and sticky like cough medicine — and two packages of jam-jams. I can sit on top of the table and look out the small window at the windswept ugliness of Elsinore just beyond.

I force myself to chew so I won't choke, but there is no real cognitive objective. Mainly I am palming the cookies into my mouth while thinking of nothing at all, and that's the beauty of it: while thus occupied I can think of nothing. My mother cannot loom up and steal my thoughts, nor am I able to worry obsessively, unrelentingly, as if digging in my own wounds. In, push it in, chew hard to manufacture sufficient saliva to swallow it all, even the congealed lumps inside my cheeks. There is comfort here amongst the cans and bottles, amid the stacks and buckets and boxes and bags. There will always be this, if there is nothing else at all for me, there is at least this, and this is something that she cannot take away from me. I will admit to a selfish pleasure: perhaps she was saving the cookies for Joss.

The second part of the equation is no harder than the first, except that when I creep along the hallway to the bathroom, I hear Joss in there: grunting and spitting, coughing with a croupy, deep-chest rattle. I cannot fathom what my mother sees in him or how she can allow this person in such proximity. With him as close as this, there can be no escape at all from his vile thereness. With him as close as this, she can see the pores in his skin, smell his sweat, be privy to his distasteful heat.

I am forced to do it outdoors behind the house, and I do, ramming my fingers down my throat a time or two to start things moving. This takes some effort because I imagine I'm not easily repulsed, and because I cannot disgorge my own punishment as easily as I'd like. It would be childish of me to admit I enjoy this, vomiting behind my mother's house. I'm sure someone has developed some sort of theory about it, about what I am actually doing, what scenarios I am enacting, how my resentment of my mother manifests itself. Hardly as exciting as the Oedipal drama but compelling nonetheless.

When I go back inside the house, they are sitting at the table eating as if nothing has occurred. Joss eats with the stolid regularity of a machine, his fork rising and falling; I imagine that he fucks the same way. My mother is smoking a cigarette, something I have never seen her do before. Are the people with whom I must consort in this life somehow archetypes of me, do I unconsciously gather versions of them around me over and over again? If so, then my mother is merely another facet of myself, and I of her. Thus we are inextricably bound by our invisible navel string.

I think about all the times I have been through this crucible — with her and with myself. It is true, you know. Whatever doesn't kill you will make you strong and hard, so hard inside that nothing can ever touch you again, nothing can ever hurt you again. You can be impervious to anything, as unyielding as a rock, scabs like barnacles over the wound. You will expect nothing and receive nothing; you will know no comfort.

It is an austere life but not without its satisfaction.

You watch now — she's gone off back to St. John's in a huff. I knows her, I knows her like the back of my jesus hand. Like it's any of her business what I does. Like she got any call to look at me like that. I seen the way she looked at me, and the way she looked at Joss — like he wasn't fit to scrape off the bottom of her boots.

Blood of a bitch went out the back and eat up all me jam-jams that I was saving for Joss. I can't have nothing with her around, I never could. I wish she'd stay out to St. John's instead of coming here all the time, pestering me and poking her nose in.

She got no idea about Joss, all she thinks about is Jack. I hates to be stirring up the past, but I got to tell her, I suppose. How in the name of God am I going to say something like that? I was never any good at talking about stuff to her. She's just like . . . she's just like Jack, although I don't know how that's possible. She's just like Jack was. She gets hurt right easy, and you can't say anything to her, even now, and she a grown woman. She used to get right hurt over nothing when she was small, and you couldn't talk sensible to her, because she'd put her face up all hard, like, and make out there was nothing wrong. Jack used to cater to her all the time, *What's the matter, my love? Tell Daddy.* But she'd argue with him that it was all right. I don't know how come she was like that.

Joss and I haven't spoke properly, and he haven't asked me or anything, but I don't mind if he stays over here to the house. There's plenty of room for his clothes and that in the closet, and I got a couple drawers in the bureau cleared out for him. Sure, there's no sense of him being over to the old house with Eleanor and Marion, and them like two old maids. That's no life for a man. They're Salvation Army, anyway, they don't hold with having a drop or taking a smoke, and I knows Joss likes to have a drink now and again. I don't mind en doing it. And he's happy enough with me, so where's the harm? It's not like I owes Jack anything. The only reason he ever went to the fish was because he wasn't having any truck with what was going on around here. He wasn't man enough to stand up for hisself, so he run away from it, just like Stella does. I don't know where in the name of the world she gets it to, there's no way she could have got it from Jack.

My God, I got to tell her. Perhaps I could write it in a letter and send it through the mail, do it that way. She could read it, then, and she'd know all about it. She'd know the whole thing.

If I'd known what Jack was like before I got married, I would never have married en. Of course, I never had much choice, unless I wanted to end up like Roslyn Barrett, knocked up every year or so for some fella up in Rigolet and having half-Eskimo youngsters, and he wouldn't marry her. I knowed Joss wouldn't do nothing about it, because Marion would of killed en if she knew. He was always afraid of Marion because she had a tongue on her. She'd never cuss or anything like that, they was Salvation Army, but she'd give him some tongue-banging.

Jack never knew the difference anyway.

I am driving back to my own house when it occurs to me that I hate my mother. It's not something I have ever considered in any real depth before, or even expected, come to that. It's not as if I have ever blamed her for anything, up till now. It would never occur to me to blame her for anything at all — I have always held myself entirely accountable for everything.

I take the old way back to Topsail, driving on the old cracked roads that lead back from Elsinore like corrupted veins racing away from a diseased heart. Full November now, with winter coming on quickly, and everywhere around me the wind feels as cold as death. I have stolen one of my mother's cigarettes, and I am smoking it out the open window, nearly choking on it. It reminds me of being young and stealing cigarettes from my grandfather to go and stand up on the hill behind our house and smoke them, Debbie Winsor and I, playing at sophistication and flicking our hair back over our shoulders. She married a drunk, Debbie Winsor, married a drunk who beats the shite out of her four or five times a week. I wonder what that must be like, if there is some kind of ritual to it: do they have some secret signal that each uses to alert the other to the impending assignation? *Tonight I'll beat your brains out with a two-*

by-four. It's morbid, but you wonder about things like that — I wonder about things like that. I suppose it's some kind of connection, after all. It's someone waiting there at home when you get there, it's like having a cat.

When I finally make the turn into the lane, it's very dark, and my neck and shoulders are stiff from driving. I shouldn't make the drive all in one piece like that, but I can't stop myself. I can't stop anywhere along the road from Elsinore, I have to keep going, to put it as far behind me as it can be, as quickly as possible.

I lock the car, all except the driver's door. I live in fear of being frozen out of my car some night. What if I had to go to the supermarket, and I couldn't get into my car? It doesn't bear thinking about. I'd end up like my mother and Uncle Joss: eating lobster in November, eating lobster and drinking Tetley Tea, and laughing together over things that make no sense. Some things shouldn't be funny. A man shouldn't eat lobster and drink tea with his brother's widow. It's not right.

There's mail: light bill, phone bill, water tax, a public service announcement from the town council. If I want my garbage picked up during the winter months, it has to be at the curb by eight in the morning. There's an anonymous brown envelope that I know is filled with slides of paintings — Liam, insisting that I choose the one I like best for the cover of my book. There's a fat packet of coupons: dry-cleaning, pet food, getting the siding on my house washed for half price. I pitch it into the trash and go through to the living room, turning on lights as I go. Something I love about my house is that it's old, it has a character of unabashed luxury. The mouldings are mahogany and so are the door frames; the book cases in my study are teak, polished to the silken texture of an eyelid.

The living room is cold, and I turn up the furnace, listen to the humming throb underneath my feet as it comes to life. There is something very satisfying about living alone, I think — I can have my heat any way I want it without worrying what anyone else thinks. I can do whatever I like: eat pretzels or strawberry yogurt in the bathtub, lie on the living room rug and stare at the ceiling, thinking nothing. I don't have to hear anyone else's voice or listen to anyone complaining. I could never live where people had voices, the cacophony would drown me.

The light on my answering machine is blinking, and as I draw near, I see there are two messages. In the moments the tape takes to rewind, I find myself thinking of my mother, except there's no reason for her to phone me and no reason for me to listen if she talks. I find this notion freeing.

The first call is from Liam. "We're ready to go to press, so can you tell me what you'd prefer for the cover?" His sense of timing is, as always, uncanny. "Give me a call when you get home from . . . wherever it is you've gone. Don't be a stranger, girleen." There is a pause, as if he wants to say something more, and I find myself listening to the silence, a stretch of nothing during which anything can happen. "All right," he finally says, "I'll talk to you soon." Perhaps he is worried about me; I make a mental note to call him in the morning.

The second call is from Sam. "I was thinking about what we'd talked about yesterday, and I'm worried about you. Can you call me when you get in? Reverse the charge if you like. I'll be in all evening. Jamie's coming round and we're going to watch the football." Jamie is his best friend, a sunny, blue-eyed youth who is more beautiful than any mortal deserves to be. I have seen pictures of him and Sam together, and although Sam is handsome enough, Jamie is positively blinding. I don't believe I could stand to be in his presence — the very nearness of such perfection might kill me.

Sam's voice on the tape is very crisp and clear, as if he were standing in the room or seated just behind me. If I press my eyelids very tightly shut, I can see him there, in his sloppy shirt and tattered jeans, his lanky body sprawled in the leather chair Aunt Marion used to own. *Hello, Stella . . .*

My heart is slamming into my ribs, but he's not here. There's no one here except me, and that's good, it's right and proper and correct, it's how it should be. I imagine I am befuddled with ghosts; it's Nancy again and the lighthouse at Elsinore. Perhaps I'm overtired. That's what it is. I need to sleep.

While I am running water for a bath, I lock the bathroom door and pull the blinds down over the windows. I can't bear to see my own face in the mirror, and so I drape a towel over the medicine cabinet, shutting in the reflection. I can't stand to look at her: that face, those eyes, that mouth. *You makes me sick to my stomach, you do. You — look at you. Sure, what in the name of the world is wrong with you atall? You're like something hauled through a knothole. Look at the size of ye. How am I supposed to get clothes to fit ye? Sure you're as big as the side of a house. You got a arse on ye like the broad side of a barn. I can't get nothing to fit you.*

The scale says I've gained two and a half pounds. It doesn't lie; it never has. I can feel the excess weight gathering around my ribs, and when I poke myself, my fingers feel the doughy texture of guilt. *Sitting there, stuffing candies in yer mouth, and you the size you are. You makes me sick, you do. I feels like I wants to run away. Sure, I got to be seen in public with you. How do you think I feels? You sitting there up to the Sunday school picnic like a starved gutted gull, eating ice cream and I told ye, if I told ye once . . . but nothing gets through your head. Me then, working me arse off, scoating me guts out for you.*

When I get into the bath, I feel heavy as a stone, as if the bathtub were the bottom deepness of a well, dark and dripping. I want to swirl down the drain when I let the water out, but instead I sit there while the tub empties, heavy as lead.

I must begin the whole thing over again tonight. I make this promise to myself all the time, it's like dancing alone, promenading in the kitchen with a broom. No food for a week, just hot water with lemon in it and a packet of Sugar Twin if I like. I can have gum, but only the sugarless kind. I can have all the water I want. I know from experience that I will require vast amounts of water, enough to float a battleship at least, or a whale.

You're going on a diet, Missy. I'm not having you going around here the summer — look at yourself. I'm ashamed to look at ye. The size of ye. Haven't you got no shame? Surely you must know what ye looks like, or haven't ye got any eyes in yer head? Of course, I always knew you were stun — stun as me arse, and that's the truth. Just like Jack's crowd, they're all queer in the head. No, she don't want a glass of syrup, she got to lose weight. The doctor says she's too heavy.

There always was an out that Mother never knew about, thank God. I was fourteen when I discovered how to have my cake and eat it. Aunt Marion arranged for me to go to Salvation Army camp with some of the other girls in Elsinore, and a very tall, very thin girl with dishwater blonde hair took several of us into the toilets and showed us how to get rid of something we'd eaten. Once I got used to it, I didn't mind, and it was very easy; I lost weight at an alarming pace and became so adept that I could literally eat whatever I wanted. If my mother noticed the bleeding gashes on my knuckles, she never mentioned it. It became a contest between us to see who could lose the most weight.

It was a kind of exile, when all was said and done. It still is.

I think about looking at my body in the mirror, so as to impress myself with what has to be done, but I don't believe I could stand it.

CHAPTER SIX

I keeps thinking about it. Joss is gone to bed, and I'm still up, sot here by meself at the table, having a smoke. I shouldn't be touching the fags — this is what killed my father — but there's something to it. While I'm having a fag I can relax for a minute. I haven't got to go thinking about old foolishness.

I can see meself, reflected in the window. I looks just like my mother, now, and that's the truth. I never in me life thought I'd end up looking like Mother, but I do.

I remember when I was young, when Mother would be in the San, and I'd go up in their bedroom while Father was out and look around at things. The ceiling in the bedroom was right low, I remember that, now, you almost had to duck your head when you was walking around it, but of course, that was only in me mind.

Mother had this real shiny bedspread that she brought over from Scotland when she come over to marry Father — a dark, plummy colour, like dried blood, and soft to touch, like skin. I never seen a bedspread like it. You could lift up the corner of it and turn it back and forth, and it seemed to change colours, and when you'd lie down on it, it felt cold, like water.

Mother had a medical book that she brought with her, too, a great big heavy one about four inches thick, with a dark red leather cover. It had all kinds of pictures in it: men with bandages around their heads, like in the war, and little youngsters with bits of stuff in their eyes, and this woman made out of glass, you could see her insides, even see the baby she was carrying inside of her. I never knew where babies come from until I was older. Once when she had some of the church ladies over for tea (this was before she went in the San) I came downstairs with the book and asked her what the picture was. Well! She like to died, now, and that's the truth. How come youngsters are always asking about things — things they're better off not knowing?

Stella never asked me about anything. I don't remember her asking me anything. She used to ask Jack — used to torment the living daylights out of him, always asking, *Daddy, how come?* I don't know how he put up with it. God forgive me, but the youngster used to drive me to distraction.

I'm not young anymore. I can see that now, looking at meself in the window. I looks like my mother did when she was my age. I can put on all the makeup I likes, dye me hair, I knows I'm not young. Lord Jesus, I knows it. I'm lucky Joss don't care about all that. He's not fussy like Jack was.

I should go up and see what kind of headstone Stella got for Jack.

When Mother was in the San, there was only me and Father in the house. Father come back shell-shocked from the war, and he never said much anyway — that's what the Bristows were like, they were right close-mouthed, the whole works of 'em. Sure, Nita Bristow is my cousin and she don't even open her mouth to me over to the store. Father was like that right up until the day he died, he hardly said a word unless it was to complain about something. He could get some crabby if he didn't like the way the dinner was cooked: *Your mother don't burn the potatoes like you do.* I'd be that embarrassed, I could bawl. I was thirteen, for God's sake, and my mother in the San with TB in the spine.

I remember when I first got me period, I was about fifteen, I suppose. Girls didn't start till later on, back then, not like now, with the little ones getting it when they're eight or nine. Sure, that's not natural. The world is gone, anyway. It's all gone to Hell in a hand-basket.

I knew what it was because I read about it in the medical book that Mother had. I used to hide the book under me bed and read a bit every night before I went to sleep. I thought I wanted to be a nurse when I got older, but Mother said I never had enough brains to be a nurse, and I'd be better off finding some man to marry me. I read in the book how young women would start to bleed, and that meant you were ready to start having youngsters. Eva and I used to hide away up in our camp up in the woods and look at the pictures in the book. That's how I learned what men had and how you got youngsters. Mother never told me nothing.

I woke up one morning and I felt right sick to my stomach. My God, I thought I was going to die. When I went to the toilet and pulled my pants down, there was blood all over 'em. Well, I knew then, I knew I had *it*. I went downstairs and Father was there, having his smoke at the table. I had to put a facecloth in me underpants because I had nothing else, and I went in to Eva's house and asked her if she had any Kotex. Of course, they didn't have the ones that stuck on to your pants, only the old belts with the hooks, and you put that around your waist and made do with it the best you could. Then me and Eva went out to Fifield's store, and Eva said you had to ask Ruby Fifield for a box of sweet biscuits.

Of course, the men were all there, stood around talking and picking their teeth. Ruby had this big fluffy cat, about twenty pounds it was, and it was up on the counter walking all over the bologna, enough to turn your stomach. Eva said she bought a slice of bol-ogna off Ruby once and when she turned it over to peel it, it had cat-claw marks in it. Eva said she nearly threw up. "I wants a box of sweet biscuits," I said to Ruby. She was sot down behind the counter on a stool, reading *True Confessions* with her glasses on a string around her neck. I don't know how she could read like that. When I asked her, she looked up and chewed her gum at me for a minute.

"Sweet biscuits?" She said it loud enough for the men to hear, and Headley Tuck turned around and winked at me and Eva. "How's ya gittin' on, me trout?" he said. Mother said Headley was so stupid that his mother must've had en for her own brother.

Thank God Eva was there, or I would have died. Ruby reached under the counter and wrapped something up in a sheet of brown paper that she hauled off the big roll on the counter. "That's fifty cents," she said, and put her hand out for it. Luckily Father had give me a few cents, or else I don't know what I would have done.

She was never a real mother to me, even after she come back from the San. God forgive me, but I never had a mother. She was that hard, look — she was that hard, she was as hard as nails to me.

I don't know what Stella is always whining about. I wasn't hard to her like that, not like my mother was to me. Anyway, youngsters got it too easy nowadays. They runs the grownups, and you're not allowed to lay a hand on 'em. Oh no, that's child abuse.

Stella never minded a bloody thing I said to her — I used to have to clout her to make her listen, she was that stun. She was always off in a world of her own, just like Jack's crowd.

I should have said something about Joss when she was here. Aye, it's easy enough to think it. I'm not good at talking about stuff, my mother never talked to me about nothing. I think everybody is gone right cracked, always wanting to talk about stuff.

My God, though, I got to tell Stella. I knows we don't get along, but I got to say something. I figured having Joss here in the house might give her some idea, but of course she always takes everything the wrong way. I can't say nothing to her, she's that soft-hearted, everything gets to her. What's I going to do? *I'm your mother, Stella, and I wants to tell you something.* I'm no good at talking to her, I never was.

I'll get the writing tablet and write a little note to her, put it in the mail. That's the best thing to do.

I think I'll have another smoke before I goes to bed, Joss is already asleep. I gets lonely sometimes, here in the house. I never ever had a close friend to talk to, although I wished I did. If Eva was still alive, it might be different, but she's been dead these five years. It's hard to believe, that: I seen her over to the cottage hospital one day and the next day Charlotte Tuck phoned me to say that Eva was being waked over to the Salvation Army. My best friend in school, when we were youngsters, and then she was dead and gone, just like that, in her casket, sure, shrivelled up like a old woman, gone away to nothing, and her face all sunk in. She was the same age as me. It's hard to believe — breast cancer. I remembers when she first had it, she phoned me one afternoon. I was wiping the floor with a bit of hot soapy water and the phone rang. "I suppose you heard I got to have me titty off," she said. Of course, Eva smoked then, too. I couldn't go and see her in to the hospital, she went to St. John's to have it done, in to the Grace. They had to take all of it, the breast, the muscle and under her arm. God knows, now, she suffered like a dog, and then they said it was too late anyway, 'twas gone all through her. When she come home I carried up a few chocolates to her — she was staying with her sister Jeannette. Her arm was swole up and she looked some bad.

I was happy when I was young, me and Eva used to have a bit of fun. Sometimes when I'm here by meself I minds I'm talking to her. "Eva," I'll say, "let's have a cup of tea now," and I'll go and put the kettle on.

I must be losing me mind.

At some point, I always have to go out somewhere, whether it's back to Elsinore or to buy food, I have to go out. I hate going out, it's something I utterly despise, I never feel as naked as I do in public, unprotected from the judgement of all those other eyes open to their gazes. They're all looking at me, measuring me against themselves, all the while knowing that I'm not as good as they are, that I can never be as good as they are.

When I was little, I used to walk to school every morning by myself unless the weather was bad, and then Uncle Joss would take me down the long road to the middle of Elsinore, driving very slowly in his old brown Impala with the plastic shower curtains on the seats. I used to sneak sideways glances at him, at his round cheeks and his snub nose, his pale blue eyes, and wonder who he reminded me of. His stomach was round and fat, like a teddy bear's, and he had plump little hands like my Sunday school teacher. He used to bite his nails a lot, but never when he was driving. When he was driving he'd clamp both hands on the wheel and stare straight ahead through the windshield. Sometimes he'd bite his bottom lip — I expect that's where I've gotten it from.

I can't hate him, no matter how much I want to, and then I think I should hate him, and I try to manufacture some festering, steaming, barely turned resentment, but I can't. He's so harmless-looking: stout and smiling, with pale blue eyes and button nose and rosy cheeks like Santa Claus. What the hell does he see in my mother? Doesn't he realize she'll eat him alive?

I have to go out today and get the things I need. I've made a list of everything; I must replenish my supplies before the weather turns and winter sets in. I can't be in the house in January, the cold and endless months that follow Christmas, without supplies. It's not possible.

I never go to the stores here; I usually drive into St. John's and choose a grocery store at random, never the same one twice. The cashiers tend to give you strange looks if you frequent the same place and purchase items in such large quantities. After a while, you inhabit that discrete space in the shopgirl brain: *weirdo*. And you inhabit it along with the old Scottish schoolteacher with whiskey on his breath and melted purple socks, and Brad the Hockey Captain with his smelly sweater. I have to choose my venue carefully so I will not be categorized. There are so many things to think about, there's so much I have to do. I can't simply go, like other people. I always have to make sure I'm ready for the trip, apart from things like money and lists and wondering whether there's enough gas in the car. Another woman would check her hair and makeup at the door.

Because the air is raw, and because it is late autumn, I decide to go into St. John's rather than out to Carbonear or Harbour Grace as I have done on previous occasions. But before stepping out the door, I must prepare.

In the back of my closet, hidden underneath the heavy winter coats, my graduation gown and the wedding dress I bought and never wore, is a selection of men's clothes. Not smooth business suits, not elegant sports wear, but black jeans, a few handsome sweaters, cowboy boots, a leather jacket that clings to my body like wet chamois. None of it means anything, does anything, if I am wearing a bra and panties underneath. Any actor will tell you that one must create the illusion from the inside, and I do: my breasts carefully bound with an elastic bandage, a singlet, cotton boxer shorts. It's easy enough. I keep a room in my house especially for this purpose, so I can become him — the man I would be if I were a man and had that freedom to come and go, that freedom to be who I wished. When I go into this room to dress, to become this man that I am not, it feels as though I'm an intruder in my own house, as if I'm poking about in his things while he is away. There is a bed in this room — the bed he would sleep in if he existed — and when I lie down upon it, I feel foreign in my skin.

I even know what he looks like; he looks nothing at all like me, even though he is what I become. My eyes are blue or maybe green, I'm never sure, but he has one brown eye and one blue eye. Although his hair is dark like mine and shoulder-length and wavy, his has a certain gleam to it, not so much hair as a glossy pelt. His skin is very white, the skin of someone who shuns the light of day, who stays indoors. If I touched his cheek it might tear like paper, he is that fragile.

There is envy inherent in cross-dressing, although some would argue that it isn't really cross-dressing when a woman merely wears men's clothes. We only ever envy what we see every day: the man who comes and goes when he likes, who picks up his hat in his hand and walks away, or runs away, or goes to sea for months or years at a time. The woman is strictly stationary, goes nowhere. She might as well be a nail driven into the wall.

I spent a lot of time looking out the window when I was a child. I expected I would see my father coming home, striding over the hills like a figure out of Robert Louis Stevenson, braving the elements, returning triumphant. There was an idea of romance that was tied up with him and what he did when he was away from the house. It was probably more interesting than what my mother did, immobile inside the house. When I consider it this way, I begin to understand how she could be so miserable, so constantly dissatisfied. Perhaps in the beginning she had dreams for herself, just as I had. Perhaps she did the only thing she could think to do. Perhaps that's why I'm here. She never did realize what she was doing, as far as I am concerned. I was her means of escape, but after they were settled into their lives with each other, after he had gone once more to the sea that keened about his ears like a whore, she must have understood. She must have understood that she couldn't send me back the way she'd return a pair of defective boots bought out of the catalogue. I was here to stay, I was part of her landscape, I was the everlasting reminder of her own folly. And yet I remember the times when she pointedly ignored me, even if I was right there in the room, as if to erase me from the vicinity and thus from her consciousness.

Impossible, then, that I should move about the world in the weak body of a woman. If I am to exist in their spaces, I must present myself in a form that is more acceptable to them. This is the most fundamental kind of shape-shifting there is: every time I go out into the world, I leave myself behind, like a shed skin upon a beach, a discarded pelt, a warning.

When I get into the car, I am transformed: I've made myself into him. His gestures are different from mine, he is more confident, more sure of his place in the world. He's my father as a young man and also some creature I have never seen in life but have only glimpsed around the borders of my consciousness, a mythic being who has inhabited the dark landscape of my dreams. He isn't afraid to go into a store and buy the things he needs. No one will dare to question him. He is male and can roam about the world as he chooses.

I find a small supermarket in the middle of the city. I'm not sure why I choose this one particularly, only that I do. There is something about it that feels safe to me, as if I might be left alone in here, not noticed, certainly not commented on as if I were some kind of usurper. It's one of those so-called family supermarkets, like the old Easy Save that my mother used to frequent when I was a child in Elsinore: small, narrow wooden shelves no more than shoulder height, rickety shopping carts and a bakery rack conspicuously placed beside the door. Someone had obviously seen the advantage in displaying the valuables thus; laid out in glistening rows, they shone with an unhealthy pallor, a patina of grease. If you're going to eat a lot of something, it's probably not going to be Brussels sprouts. If you're that sort of person and you're going to eat a lot of something, it's going to be pies, cakes, chocolate, ice cream. The people that run grocery stores know this, it's us they cater to, they've built an entire industry around us.

I fill my cart swiftly, salaciously, as though I were closeted here alone with all these glistening cans and gleaming bottles, everything available to my hunger. I walk like a man, my energy concentrated in the centre of my body, around the navel and not the hips. I walk with my shoulders held straight across the clavicles, with no sway or movement in them; I swing my hands at my sides in a slightly simian gesture or else jam them into my pockets, and I regard packages and boxes with masculine disdain. I toss things into my cart without seeming to look at the labels; I am slavering inside. It will take far too long to get out of the store and into my car, where I will at least be able to tear open a box or two, destroy the shiny wrapping and devour whatever is inside. For now, I must maintain the decorum I have established and be the man I have scrupulously created. I owe that much to him, and to myself.

I come to this place with the kind of idolatry that pilgrims reserve for their shrines. Here, in the midst of this shimmering plenty, I feel cleansed, as though I had gained for myself some kind of salvation.

When I pay for it and take it out into my car, I shiver with something paramount to sex or any other mundane human desire. I wait until I am some distance away, and then I can't stand it anymore. I park the car behind a Kentucky Fried Chicken, and I delve into the ice cream with my hands. The cold numbs me to the bone, but I force myself onward in spite of it, cramming the creamy stuff into my mouth until I am nearly gagging, ice cream dripping from my lips and dropping into my lap in dark brown globules. I catch sight of myself in the side mirror: a thin young man, forcing ice cream into his mouth with both hands, his chin coated with dark stickiness, his eyes huge.

When I have eaten it all, I open the door, and, leaning far out so that I am suspended over the dirty asphalt, I drop my lower jaw as far as it will go and press my index finger against the back of my tongue. It goes easier than it has at other times: ice cream is easily vomited, with little strain. After a while, you learn which things go down and which come up. The thin blonde girl at summer camp advised against spaghetti: too much opportunity for the strands to get entangled, and heaven knows, people who do this sort of thing never take the time to chew their food. The object is to push it in as fast as possible, before anything begins to surface, before anything that might implicate anyone is revealed.

When I straighten up, the young man is watching me from the rear-view mirror, tears standing in his eyes. I whisper to him, in my mother's voice: *You makes me sick. Sure, look at ye — you're blowed up like a gurnet.*

I can drive home now, the strain abated, healed and dissipated by the one act that can render me immediately sane. I am grateful for the thin blonde girl, thank God for her. I wonder where she might be now, what has happened to her in my absence.

When I get home, there is a message from Liam; it's as if he knows, as if he can predict what I will do. How did he get to know me so well, when everything I am and everything I do is calculated to push him away, keep him at a safe distance? He sounds as resolutely cheerful as he always does. I don't know how he manages it. I listen to him on the answering machine while taking off the bandage binding my breasts, then I rewind the tape and listen to it again. I like the sound of his voice — I readily admit this. I call up his image, for Liam is handsome. Why isn't he married, why doesn't he seem to have attached himself to some woman willing to carry his seed? That's what men all want, someone to carry on their names, to carry their seed. It's the only reason they're ever interested in us, as wombs, as receptacles. I have never really been in love, and if God is merciful, I will never have to be. I don't think I could stand it; it would be like my mother and Uncle Joss, the terrifying presence of each other, inescapable as your own breath and just as close, just as cloying. I don't know how people stand each other like that. Being in someone's sight all the time would drive me barking mad.

You'll never guess what I done. Honest to God, I got to be losing my mind, now, and that's the truth.

I went in and got that dress that my mother had made for me when I was fourteen, that blue one with the netting underneath. My God, I forgot how it looked. Sure, it looks just like I bought it the other day. Mind you, it's old-fashioned now, but it's still the same lovely colour as it was when I got it, it haven't faded a bit. I took real good care of it, always put it up in the closet on a hanger with garbage bags over it. That's to keep the dust off, and you can't let a dress like that in the sunlight, that's what fades it.

I remember when Stella was small, she used to love to look at the Eaton's catalogue. "Look at the ladies," she used to say. I'd get her sot down on the floor with the catalogue, and my son, she'd read through that with her fingers in her mouth — you'd think she'd never seen the like in her life. You'd think, now, the way people dressed in there and the kinds of clothes they had, that they lived on the moon. That's the God's truth, I'm sure that's what she thought. Of course, Stella never had brains enough to blow her nose. "What's that they got on?" she'd ask me, like she never seen women wearing slacks before. "How come she got that on?" If it wasn't for that catalogue, she'd have me drove. I minds when she was a teenager in high school, she used to love to order clothes out of the catalogue, though she was always hard to fit, Stella, and then she lost a whole pile of weight when she was in grade eleven. I thought she was sick first, God forgive me, I thought she had cancer. There was cancer in Jack's family — his grandmother had it in the breast, and that's how she died — so it wouldn't have surprised me, now, if that's what was wrong with Stella. I didn't know if I should take her to the doctor or not. Sure, even if you got cancer, they can't do anything for ye, can they? I don't think they can, it's something they thought up, now, to get money out of you, for drugs and whatnot. They never did nothing for poor old Eva, and her over there to the Salvation Army, getting waked, all dried up like a old woman.

God forgive me, I thought Stella might have the cancer. When she was in grade eleven, she got right skinny all of a sudden . . . I think it was round about grade eleven. She got right skinny and wouldn't eat nothing, and of course Jack was gone all the time, out on the water, or else he would of give her a good talking-to. That's all she needed was a man to straighten her out. I should of got Joss to come up to the house and blare at her, straighten her out. She got right skinny and wouldn't eat anything I cooked. Didn't that burn me up. "You'll bloody well eat," I told her, "when you gets hungry enough, you'll eat it." Mind you, she could of got up in the middle of the night and went poking around in the fridge, she was as bad as that. I never put nothing past Stella — she never fooled me. All she done that whole year was stay in her room all the time. God only knows what she was at in there, and I don't care, now. She never had no friends over to the high school. She never mixed with any of the other girls. She wouldn't mix with no one, always stuck in her room reading old foolishness in library books. "Stella, what in the name of God are ye at in there?" I asked her once. "Writing a novel," she said, right saucy-like, and I could of smacked the mouth off of her. I used to take up a bit of supper for her and put it in the oven, and it'd stay there till kingdom come, all dried up, a lovely bit of cabbage and onions, new potatoes my father grew down in the garden. She wouldn't eat none of it. Used to drink water all the time. I think she had the worms, myself, because I used to hear her in the bathroom all hours of the night, throwing up, and they says when people got worms, that's what they does. She said to me once, "I makes meself throw up three or four times a day." I said, "Sure, that's foolishness. Wasting food — you should be ashamed of yourself." And then she said, in that way she used to have, right saucy, "It's called *bulimia*, Mother." She was right proud of it, back-answering me like that. I suppose she looked it up in one of them old medical books my mother had. It was just like Stella to be at the like of that. Mind you, I don't see nothing wrong with trying to watch your figure. I always kept an eye on myself, never let myself get too big. But what Stella done, that was taking it too far.

I got this dress took out, now, the same dress I wore to the dance when I was fourteen. I'll never forget it, the way all the boys lined up by the wall to dance with me. The other girls were some jealous, let me tell you, and them all done up like hoors. They never had a dress so nice as mine.

It still fits me. I tried it on last night after Joss went on to bed, just to see. It still fits, now, after all these years. I still got me figure.

Jack never liked me in this dress — he didn't hold with women wearing shiny clothes, he said. He said if God wanted us to wear shiny dresses and be prideful like that, we'd all be lying around on cushions like the Sheik of Araby. Jack had queer ideas, sometimes.

If Joss asks me to marry en, I think I might wear this dress. Joss wouldn't say nothing about me wearing this, sure, and I loves the colour of it. Pale blue it is, with a greenish tinge to it, like the water looks when you're in a boat, or in them little puddles down the beach when the tide goes out. I always loved that colour. Some people likes red or beige, but not me. I likes this colour.

Would we get married over to the church? No, they'd not shut up about that, the Fifields and them, their bloody tongues wag from now to doomsday. We'll get married here in the house, just the two of us. I'll have the United Church minister over. Never mind what Marion thinks, if she had it her way, we'd all get married in the Salvation Army in the black uniforms, like a funeral.

I likes to have a man around the house. I don't mind saying it. I likes having Joss here so I got someone to lie next to. I was always afraid of the dark.

I minds one time when Jack and I were courting, and he was

gone out to the fish, and Joss come up over the garden one evening and asked my mother if I wanted to go walking with en. "She's not fit to go walking with you or any man," she said. Of course, I knew what she bloody well meant, my mother. She had that way about her. She never cared about anyone's feelings.

Me and Joss went over to the old lighthouse. It was a lovely evening, just after getting dark, so it must have been past mid-summer. It might have been August or September, I don't know for sure. It was right warm outside, and I wasn't starting to show. He wouldn't put his arm around me or nothing like that, because of Jack, and we didn't want people talking.

I would have done whatever he wanted, if he wanted me to go with en, I would have. Joss had a nice face, he still do, he's right kind-looking. Jack was a nice-looking man in his way, but he was always somewhere else in his mind. Even when he was here in the house, it was like he'd rather be somewhere else, like he was thinking about other things. Joss is always listening to me when I talks. He even asks me what I thinks about things. Not like Jack, Jack used to tell me and that was it. He knew what he was talking about and I never. Sure, he could hardly read and write, for God's sake, and him telling me, then. Yes, I know now.

We went up to the lighthouse, me and Joss. Oh my, it was a nice night. I had me cardigan over me shoulders, but I never needed it, not really. The wind was soft, and I was glad to be with Joss. I felt like I had everything in the world I wanted just then: to be walking on the downs with Joss, and the lovely warm wind. It was like something out of a book, sure.

We went inside the lighthouse, the door was unlocked even though the keeper wasn't home. He had nothing in there to steal. Everybody knew he was a hermit, and me and Joss weren't going to steal what he had, didn't want what he had.

We went inside, and Joss told me all about the light: how it was run and what it run on and what made it go around. We went up the stairs to the top, but I couldn't look in the light — it made me sick, going around like that. I told Joss I felt like I was going to throw up, and he put his arm around me, he's good that way. I liked having his arm around me and him holding on to me. "We don't want you getting sick," he said, "on a nice night like this." He never mentioned anything about me being the way I was. He never said a word. He was a real gentleman, Joss. He still is, sure.

I never loved Jack, now, and that's the truth. I looks back and wonders how in the name of God I ended up where I am: Jack dead and gone, Stella . . .

At least I got Joss.

CHAPTER SEVEN

There's an empty aquarium in the hallway in my mother's house, filled with beach rocks. I remember carting buckets of water from the harbour to fill it, when I was about nine or ten, because I wanted Sea Monkeys. I'd seen them advertised on the back of a comic book: tiny people with crowns, living in a magical underwater world, sitting on chairs and eating at tables. They were completely nude save for an artfully drawn ruffle about each of their necks, their feet were webbed like the flippers of seals, and they displayed absolutely no external genitalia. This was compelling, seeing as how there were two smaller Sea Monkeys in the illustration, a boy and a girl, both wearing ruffles like miniature Elizabethan courtiers, both naked.

Breathlessly, fearing the outcome, I sent away my ninety-five cents and waited in horrible anticipation by the window every day for a month, watching for the post office truck. Although it was considered mannerly to wait at least an hour for Pansy to unpack the mail, I was out of the house like a shot. It had arrived: a slender, flat package postmarked San Francisco, California.

They looked nothing like the illustration on the back of the comic book. If anything, they looked like the sea lice on lobsters and crab: tiny transparent creatures appearing slowly out of the strange dust I stirred into the tank. My mother went by, bearing a load of wet laundry in a basket. "What in the name of the world is that?" she asked. "Did you waste your money on the like of that? Sure, you're cracked."

Her reaction was the same as her cold, clinical touch when she washed me: standing me on a chair in front of the kitchen sink, the cold drafts from the leaky window making me shiver, sending bolts of static through me. My skin felt exquisitely sensitized, as if her fingers communicated her distaste to me and I was obliged to respond to it. She always put too much soap on the cloth, and the bubbles burst on my skin with a prickling sensation, like pins and needles. She would scrub me rapidly, eager to get it done, and all the while her face would be set, hard, distant. I could almost hear her thoughts: *I don't know why you can't do this yourself, big girl like you. Sure, you're old enough to wash yourself now. I don't know why I got to do it. I got better things to do.*

When she washed me down below, as she put it, she would be especially hurried, rapid and harsh, her fingers digging into me, sweeping soap into my body's cavities until it burned like acid. "Now go and put your pyjamas on," she'd say. "And brush your dirty teeth. You looks like something no one owns."

She'd go into the living room then and turn on the television, glad to have it over and done with, glad to be shut of it — of me.

I don't know why I'm thinking of Sea Monkeys, that old aquarium or my mother. I am sitting at my kitchen table in the middle of the day with a series of slides spread out on the smooth wooden surface.

Mostly what I want to do is look out the window. The sky is raw and ragged-looking, with tails of old clouds straggling by on the wind's invisible hook. I like the way the naked trees appear, pressed against the sky as if seeking entry; the tall one just across the way rocks gently in the throes of a breeze. Liam wants me to look at pictures.

The first handful of slides are all of a piece: scurrilous, visceral, carved into the canvas as with the tip of a knife. Here and there, I can see where the artist has layered the paint on especially thick, or where her brush or perhaps her fingernail has dug into the surface, scraping to get at what is underneath. There are typical New-foundland scenes, something she has started doing recently: impressionistic boats moored at impossible wharves, boats rising out of bloody waves, a bishop walking on the water, carrying a gaff.

Then this: a young man's head with long hair streaming, drowned-looking, his eyes half-blinded like the eyes of a dying seal, a line of varicoloured spots marching in procession down his cheek, disappearing into his neck.

I recognise his face, for he is me: he is the young man I become in order that I may move about in the world, the guise I assume, the guide I embrace.

This is a joke. Liam has done this purposely.

So this is how it comes back to me, this is how I am haunted. Liam must be on to me, he must have discovered what it is I do when I go out. Perhaps he had me followed, or perhaps he follows me himself out of some misplaced devotion.

I go through to the living room and pick up the remote, switch the television on: riots in Malaysia, people screaming in the streets; an airplane crash outside of Oklahoma City; a horrible train accident in London. I think about Sam — does he take the train? It would be typical for something horrendous to occur right now, now, when I am watching, when it has my attention, when it knows me.

He must have followed me. He must have. I can't stop watching the pictures on the television: people being carried out of the train, twisted into grotesque shapes by the force of the collision, as if they had run at full speed into a wall.

The phone rings. Obsessed as I am at this moment by fragments of horror, I do not hear it. Eventually the machine picks up, and I hear my own disembodied voice, weak and wan, as if I'm speaking from the bottom of a hole or a well: *I'm not here. Please leave a message and I will return your call.*

I hear Liam: "Stella, have you looked at them bloody pictures yet? Because if you don't tell me which one you want, the art department will go ahead without you." He sounds irritated; I hear his voice and feel my scalp prickle with some emotion I don't recognise or acknowledge.

I wait until he hangs up, and then I erase the message. Somewhere behind me, a British voice is calmly unrolling the fabric of terror: fifteen dead, another forty injured, the train a mass of pretzelled metal. I am grateful to this British voice and the fact that there is order in the world. Things sometimes happen even when I am watching them, and I'm relieved.

I find myself circling back towards the picture until I am standing over the table gazing down at it. The resemblance is uncanny; it is indeed the young man I become, but it is more true. One blue eye, one brown eye, pale skin as fragile as wet paper, the line of spots marching down to vanish into his collar. *Gone to get a selkie skin to wrap the baby bunting in.* He is a man turning into a seal.

Don't go down by the water. Do you hear me? Don't you let me catch you down by the salt water. You'll get some hammering if I do.

I choose that picture for the cover of the book. I realize I like the way the young man looks, the fearlessness of him, the beauty of his expression. He will fit the new book perfectly. He is something not human. He is like me.

After all these years, I cannot fathom what my mother is afraid of.

I telephone Liam at his office and tell him I have decided which picture I want on my book. "It's that selkie one, isn't it?" I wonder aloud how he knows this, but that's Liam — he just knows things. I sometimes think he should have been a psychologist or a fortune teller. "Na, na, I've got you all figured out, so I have." Then he admits that it's his choice as well, that picture, although he does not tell me his own reasons for choosing it. I assume — perhaps incorrectly — that they have nothing to do with my own. Liam is very visual, and he probably feels its inherent aesthetic. He also has an acute sense of what works well on a book cover, and for this I am grateful. I know how much I owe Liam, to the very last penny; I have calculated it hundreds of times in my head, and I don't ever allow myself to forget what he has given me.

The books I write are not in any way savage, cruel or heartless. The mothers are always benign, Anglicized creatures, exemplars of Britannic rectitude, models of good taste, who nibble daintily at scones and sip tea amidst a sea of tweed. I have tried to write my mother as she really is, and I can't do it. I'm afraid of her, and this fear grows and gnaws at me in much the same fashion as my hatred of her sits like a stone in my throat. I'm afraid of what I might do to her; I'm afraid I might hurt her, damage her irreparably. If I killed her, I could never forgive myself. Even if I injured her unintentionally, the knowledge of my betrayal would sit badly with me. Some animals eat their young — my mother did.

I can bring myself to hate her only sometimes, when I am close to her, experiencing her intimately. When I am far away, she achieves the glow of martyrdom, and I realize how cruel I have been to judge her, how unnecessarily I have condemned her. Perhaps this is why I dream of her repeatedly, see her in my sleep: standing at the end of the hallway, belting her housecoat around her like a suit of armour, her eyes gazing straight ahead but never at me. I can never make her look at me; she never sees me. Even if I crept out of bed and went to her, knelt at her feet or patted her cheek with my hand — which would be small and childlike — she would not see me.

Liam is talking. "Stella?"

"I'm here." I wonder if I should tell him about my father. What would he think? And what would be the best way to phrase it so that he could understand? *You know my father died, right?* I could say it to him casually, as if I were discussing something benign, like the weather or the state of the world. I might slip it into our conversation as a kind of tag line, something at the end of a sentence: *Oh yeah, and my father collapsed and died a couple of weeks ago.* I have the unpleasant and socially inept habit of doing this; perhaps it is the result of my infrequent contact with others of my own species. If I were more comfortable in the presence of other people, I might not do this, but as things are, I always feel as if I have to tell them something truly shocking at the outset, like certain kinds of mental patients do. I realize I am a sitcom staple: the victim of life who loses no opportunity to relate her injuries to anyone who will listen, who digs about in her own wounds for fresh pieces of shrapnel to display. I do this unconsciously and only recognize too late what I've done.

I have not thought anything particular about my father's death, have formed no conclusions. Until now. Until this very moment, exchanging banal observations with Liam, I have not given myself the emotional space necessary to consider the plain physical fact of his demise. He no longer exists; like thistledown blown on the wind, his essence is scattered. Even now, his molecules, his atoms, the minuscule and invisible pieces of him are being dismantled by a legion of creatures who have no knowledge of him beyond the fact of his eminently reusable material. He is fodder for worms and parasites, a mere collection of substance, his body's vital fluids leaking into the ground.

I can't breathe. I feel as though I am choking. I pinch my nostrils and then release them, trying to suck air in through the too-small apertures, my physical nature desperate to overcome my psychic paralysis. I hear little choking noises, wonder if they are coming out of my mouth, wonder who might be making them.

And Liam is speaking in a language I have never heard before, a language that I recognise. It flows over me like cool water, like the pull of the sea, and I remember my dream of the whales stranded on the beach at Elsinore, dying by degrees.

"*Eiridh tonn air uisge balbh.*" His voice is a caress, a gentle hand upon the forehead, the soothing touch of a healer; I feel as though I am rocking in his arms, comforted by him. I realize that I am weeping. "Na, na, *mo chride*," he says, "Na, na." I want him to talk this way forever, because I remember — I remember Nanny Bristow slipping Gaelic into my ears when I was very little, and I remember how it comforted me.

I listen to him speaking again, and even though I know this isn't very wise, I cannot help myself. There is no one else to whom I might turn now, not even Sam, whom I love above all else. Liam is the only one who understands, but I don't even know why he understands. He simply does, and that is enough for me.

When I hang up the phone, I am still weeping, but it's good, he has released some valve in me. I leave him gently, listening as he asks if there's anything I need, anything I want. I know that if I asked him, he would come to me, he would hold me in his arms, and for a delicious, utterly terrifying moment I allow myself to consider that as a possibility before I refuse it. I know that it will be there, should I require it; Liam will be there. I am certain of it.

I never liked it here. I've always thought this is a very cold place, a very barren place, and a rugged place, and what I've had of it is a very lonely life. She's my daughter, but she never comes to see me, and for all I see of her, I might as well already be in the ground, dead and buried. If she thought I had any money, she'd be around, sure enough. But all I've got is what I've put away for my burial, to make sure.

My old man, he was buried by the Veterans because he was in the war. He died of emphysema years ago, but we always knew he would, Doctor DuZeeuw said so. He's a Boer, but they were always our people, regardless. Doctor DuZeeuw treats me like I'm his mother whenever he comes to see me. He's a lovely young man. I knitted him a sweater last winter because he had nothing warm to wear. He always says there's no one like me.

I can't see much of anything outside this window, and if my legs worked like they used to, I'd go outdoors. I can see a walkway that someone has made through the trees, just beyond the home. I always loved to walk in the woods with my poor old mother, before she got too crippled up. Towards the end of it, she was in a wheel-chair, and now I am, as well. But my mother died when she was fifty-six, and I'm long past that. I think about her sometimes, and I can see her as clear in my mind's eye as if she was standing there in front of me. She had black hair, as black as a raven's wing, and blue eyes. I had her colouring, even though my sister Nell had our father's blond hair. My mother was a real Scottish girl, she came from up in the Highlands near Aviemore, where Ted was training in the war. He went over with the Forestry first of all, and that's how he met me. He could have gone into the Canadian Army, but Ted wanted the British Army, and he ended up in the artillery. I remember when I met him at the dance. I had a lovely new suit that Nell had made over from one of my mother's old ones. Apple-green it was, with a pale yellow blouse. You couldn't get stockings, of course, there were none to be had. In the middle of the dance we heard the sirens and of course everything stopped.

It seems so long ago sometimes, and then other times it's as plain in my mind as if it was yesterday. We used to pay a penny to go to the cinema on Saturday afternoons. Later on, after everything moved down to Edinburgh, Nell and I would get the train at Waverley Station, or take a bottle of tea and a packet of sandwiches and sit in the Castle Gardens. The whole place was full of young men: Canadians and Englishmen, even Americans. The Americans always had such nice teeth, and they were such good dancers.

Nell had an American boyfriend once, from Texas, with red hair and blue eyes and freckles all over his face — Dennis, his name was. He got killed in the war. So many of them got killed in the war. When we were working at the factory, Nell and I, we'd see them in the evenings when we were on our way home, all the young men in their nice new uniforms, the sailors in their wide-legged pants, smoking on the street corners or waiting for the trains at Waverley Station. Whenever there was a dance at the canteen, they'd line up to dance, and you had to be careful to favour all of them and not just dance with one.

The Americans were the best dancers. I don't know what it was, but they could dance better than anyone. I remember one night Nell was dancing with this fellow who looked like a Spaniard but turned out to be Greek, from Crete. He was off one of the freighters, bringing supplies. He had a tattoo of a woman on his arm, and when he flexed the muscle, she'd move like she was dancing. He was after Nell to marry him for the longest time and even came to the house one Sunday afternoon, but my father gave him the heave-ho. Said he was a Freemason and there was no way his daughter was marrying a Spic. Oh, didn't Nell cry. She said he wasn't a Spic, he was Greek, but my father was having none of it. Nell didn't speak to him for weeks. She married a Polish Jew after the war and had one son before her husband went home to see his parents and disappeared. He was such a nice-looking young man, with blond hair like spun gold. A nice-looking young man.

Sometimes we'd go to the pictures with the young men who were over for training. This is where I first got to meet Ted. I think he liked to go to the pictures because they had nothing like that where he came from, and he had never seen talkies before. I remember him telling me once about how the minister of the church and the school principal brought in a silent movie and showed it in the Lodge, and how some of the older men said it was the devil's work. They were ignorant in those days, you know, not like now.

Sometimes I dream about home. A lot of the time now, when I sleep, I feel myself wandering in a kind of mist, and I can feel my father calling to me. We're going by boat to Skye, it's a trip we took once when I was seven and Nell was five. We went to Skye that summer. My mother was well for a little while — the doctor had given her gold injections, and whenever he did, she could get up from her wheelchair and walk. But it always wore off, and before long she was sick again. I can't ever mind my mother being really well. My father was away down in the mines when Nell and I were small. I remember once when we were going to see him on the train, I fell across the tracks and cut my lip. It never healed the same afterwards. My poor mother, she couldn't keep up, and she was never well.

I dream that we're going to Skye: Mother, Nell, Father and I. I can see the landscape passing by, the way the hills look in mist, purple with the heather, and the bracken brown and twisted, gold in places. The wind is cool.

I never reach Skye in the dream. I always awaken just before our little boat bumps against the shore, and it's very sad, because I want to go to Skye.

I wonder if Nell ever had that dream before she died. She's been dead five years. I remember when the letter came: her friend Margaret in Glasgow, the writing on the envelope all shaky because she was old by then. We're all old now, but we weren't always. I wonder what's become of everyone. Sometimes I find myself reaching for the pen and paper to write Nell a letter, and then I remember: she died, her heart was always bad, it was just a matter of time.

I remember when Stella was little, she used to say to me, "Nanny, tell me stories about Scotland." I bought her a book with pictures in it so she could see what it was like, and she used to cry and say she wanted to go there, only she didn't say "there," she said "home." Once when she was really small, she stayed down with me one Friday night when Jack was home and Mim wanted the house. I put her up to bed and tucked her in — she always liked the feather mattress that we had — and then I went downstairs with Ted to have a wee drink before bed, a wee glass of whisky.

About five or ten minutes later, I heard something, and bless her heart, there she was on the stairs, holding on to the railing and crying. "What's wrong, my love?" I asked her, and I wrapped her up in a blanket and brought her down to sit with me on the chesterfield. "What are you crying about? Dinnae greet."

"I wants to go home, Nanny," she said, and I thought she meant she wanted to go up to her own house with Mim, but then she said, "*No*, Nanny, I wants to go home to Scotland." It was like the child remembered something. I said to her what my poor old mother used to say to me: "You've been here before." And then I told her all about Johnny Norri and Tam Lin and the Good People and the Summerland.

I'd like to go there someday soon. I'm awful tired.

I told Joss what I wanted. I told en after we had eat our supper. I come right out and said it. I didn't want to fool around, I wanted it out in the open. *Joss,* I said, *I think if you and me are going to be living here in the one house —*

And then he cut in on me: *You wants to get married, do ye, maid?* I couldn't say anything for a minute or two, I was that surprised. *I don't know,* I said. *Do you want to, or what?* And then he said we might as well. He was kind of worried, though, he told me. He said he didn't know if it was right or not. *Jack was me brother,* he said to me. Lord Jesus, as if I didn't know that. I was some mad, but I never said nothing, and he clammed up then.

I never had a proper wedding with Jack. No, that's not true, Marion took over everything and done it the way she wanted it. Although I suppose I wouldn't have had either wedding if it wasn't for Marion. My mother didn't want me to marry Jack in the first place — didn't want me to marry at all, she said. *I'll send you to Scotland,* she said, *and you can stay with Auntie Nell and have your baby over there. Someone will take it up for adoption and then you can go and take a commercial course, learn how to type and get a good job.* Aunt Nell was a secretary in a big office in London, some kind of insurance place. She wanted me to be like Aunt Nell. *You don't want a baby at your age,* she said. *And I'm not bringing it up.*

She really took to Stella when she was small, though. I was glad. I was that wore out with having her, God forgive me, I didn't want to be bothered, and all Stella did when she was a baby was bawl. Oh my God, didn't that youngster bawl. We couldn't get her to shut up. I was that wore out, look, I could have hove her in the salt water, and that's the truth. "Go on, for God's sake," I would of said, "go and swim with the bloody seals." Enough to drive you nuts.

I'm going to wear the blue dress when Joss and I gets married. I'm going to have the wedding here in the house, and have the United Church minister over. I'm not getting married in no Salvation Army, all done up in black like a funeral.

I should tell Stella, I suppose. She's me daughter, after all, and blood is thicker than water, more or less. Of course, she'll probably bring that Irish fella, what's his name, Stephen or something. God, I hates him. My mother always said the Irish are lazy as cut dogs, drunk six days out of seven, hates Protestants. Sure, all they lives on is potatoes, like this Irish girl she knew in Edinburgh, years ago, married this Catholic fella and her with about twenty-five youngsters before she was thirty. Spent her whole day cooking spuds for that lot and changing shitty diapers. I only ever met that Irish fella once, when Jack and I were on our way into town to do a bit of shopping for Christmas, and we stopped in to Stella's house. He was there, that Stephen or Liam or Eamonn or whatever his name is. Gave me this look like I had horns in me head. Saucy bugger.

Stood there watching me, then, right quiet, not saying a word, stood close to Stella like I was going to haul off and smack her in the mouth.

I got to phone her, I suppose, and tell her.

I listen to his phone ring, even though I know he will be working — in rehearsal all day and then studying his scripts at night. I know he will be busy. I shouldn't bother him, but I can't help it. I have to tell someone.

His answerphone clicks on. "Hi, it's Sam." He's changed the message again. "Leave a message." His voice sounds terse, strained and overworked. I hang up without saying anything; I can't speak such truths to a machine, I need to tell him in person, it's not something you can say over the phone. But what is stopping me, when I tell him everything by phone, e-mail or letter? Perhaps I can save it for when he comes to Halifax. I'll probably tell him then.

It's snowing outside. It's nearly Christmas — how have I missed this? Where was I when it was becoming Christmas? Overseeing the new novel, discussing it with Liam on the phone, by e-mail. He wanted to meet for lunch to show me the cover design, but I couldn't bear it. "E-mail it to me," I said, "That's good enough."

I have Christmas gifts for Liam, ordered off the Web: a book of photographs, a series of surreal Irish landscapes, lush and green; an Aran sweater, knitted of a wool as pliable as seaweed; a crate of blood oranges, potent reminder of a childhood's worth of summer holidays spent near Barcelona. I feel I should be generous with Sam, and yet I have nothing for him, probably because I can't think of anything to give him, or, more precisely, because I have absolutely nothing that he wants.

The telephone rings while I am standing at the window contemplating the snow; just down the road, Christmas lights have begun to appear in the windows of my nearest neighbours' houses, multicoloured and vaguely threatening. "Hello?"

I tell him in staccato bursts, like gunfire: my father six weeks dead, my mother getting married again. I can't determine if this constitutes a tragedy or not. As I am talking to him, I flick the television on: a major snowstorm in New Brunswick has wiped out power to homes and schools. At least one person is dead, and I am curiously relieved. There are larger tragedies than my mother, and by concentrating on these I can divest myself of some self-pity.

"Stella. Stella, listen to me. For the love of God, listen. My mother's dead."

"Oh my God," I find myself saying, "Oh God, I'm so sorry, I'm so sorry, I didn't know . . . I . . . there was no way . . ."

"She's been dead for years." I hear him take a deep breath on the other end, the kind of quivering breath that people take — that men take — when they are trying not to cry. I've never heard a man cry before. My father never cried.

"I was a little boy," he says, "back home. Coming home from school. I'd be about six, I guess. Not more than that."

He tells me about the ambulance in front of the house, the police cars cordoning off the quiet street where his family lived, the flashing lights splashing eerily against the red brick walls, a stout fortress rising above the weathered pavement. "My da was out in the road, wearing a shirt and tie and his good work pants, the shine scuffed off his shoes. He kept walking back and forth in this little half-circle. He kept walking back and forth like that, like he'd dropped his keys and was looking for 'em. I started to run, but I was too little and my legs were too short. I had to get there before they put her in the ambulance, you see. I had to get there before they took her away for good, once they got her in there."

"What was it?" I ask this, even though I know, even though I am thinking fragments of Yeats: a car bomb, right in front of the house as she went out to post a letter. And then I ask, "What were they?"

It's important that I know this, too. I imagine Catholics do this sort of thing; I'm sure they would. I remember the stories I've heard, the things I've seen.

"Jesus God, Stella, does it matter? Sure, she's still dead in the end." This is why Liam's father and his aunt brought him and his sister to Newfoundland: a place like home, a new Ireland, a haven from their troubles.

I ask him to go to the wedding with me. I need someone there beside me, someone I can count on.

I got to take it out again and make sure it fits because I still can't believe that it do. I'm looking at meself in the mirror when Joss comes into the bedroom, sneaking up on me, like. God, I hates it when he does that. He's just like Jack was, always creeping around. "What're you doing?" he asks me, like he haven't got eyes to see what I'm doing. "You're going to be married in that, I suppose?"

I still got me figure, even after all this time. Of course, me hair tinted like this takes years off me. I thinks women got to look after theirself. Lots of women lets theirself go when they gets married. I never let meself go the first time, with Jack, and I won't be doing it now.

Marion found out about our plan afterwards. Of course Joss had to go up and tell her, although I suppose I can't really blame en, it's his sister after all. I figured she was going to make a big deal out of it, and she did, screeching and bawling like a cat in heat, clawing at herself. She's queer in the head, just like Eleanor was. They all goes that way in the end.

Anyway, I told her when she phoned, I wasn't having anything big, and I wasn't doing up a supper or anything like that. I told her that me and Joss were just going to have the minister over to say the prayers and that, and then we were going to have a bite of supper ourselves. The quicker I gets it over with, the better. Thank God my mother won't be here, that's something, anyway. I don't think I could stand it, she drives me, she do. She's even worse than Stella, and that's the God's truth.

I love the way it smells, I always have, even though you're not really supposed to, even though the air is rank with the scent of ancient flesh. My grandmother has been in here for years; she admitted herself when I was still in high school because she knew my mother wouldn't care for her when she got old and feeble, and she wasn't going to ask. My grandfather had long since died, consumed by the emphysema that rotted out his lungs and stole his breath. Nanny Bristow sold their house in Elsinore and came in here to town.

It is one day until Christmas, and I am here now on the pretext of delivering her gifts, even though the objects that I carry are things she neither wants nor needs: a tin of talcum powder, a pair of slippers, a warm nightie. I want her to be comfortable, and I want her to feel that she is at least cherished in some small measure, but how do you represent such profound longing with mere things?

I first see her from behind; today she is sitting in an upright chair beside the large window. The sun is blinding on the first fall of snow, this new snow that is the same colour as my grandmother's hair, gleaming white with silver, like precious metal or meticulously polished bone. I am astonished at how small she seems, crouched in her chair, and I remember when her irreverent, raucous laugh would greet me on summer mornings as she bicycled up to our house in Elsinore. *Come here and see Nanny, there's a guid wee babby.*

"Nanny?" I touch her on the shoulder gently; it doesn't do to startle her, since extreme age is liable to sudden physical failure, and I am not ready to lose her yet. "Nanny, it's me."

She turns to gaze at me, her eyes cornflower blue in the morning light. "Hello, my darlin'," she says. "How are ye?"

I pile the gifts into her lap, smile at her pleasure as she fingers the paper thoughtfully, seduced by the glimmery stuff, the hand-tied bows. If she notices anything strange in my male costume, she does not comment. Perhaps she thinks it's some sort of fashion, or perhaps she is too polite or too uninterested to offer an opinion. I sit beside her while she opens the parcels carefully, slitting the Scotch tape with her thumbnail, parting the paper to reveal the gift. She folds each sheet of paper and tucks it against her side. I wonder what she could possibly be keeping it for.

While she is exclaiming over her presents, I ponder how best to tell her about my mother. In the end, it is like telling Liam about my father's death: I spill it all at once.

She stares at me, but only for a few seconds, then turns away, heaves herself unsteadily to her feet. A disgusted noise curdles in the back of her throat. "Yer mither was always a wee bit soft in the head," she says. "I dinnae care what she does." This is all she will say, this is all she needs to say. She and I both know that I will be present at my mother's nuptials, if only to witness the act; she and I both know that she will be absent, having already seen everything there is to see.

When I leave, she hugs me close, and I feel the creak and grind of her old bones pressed against my flesh. "Ye're a guid girrul," she says. She turns away before my actual departure, so as to banish me from sight as very small children do; invisible to her now, I obligingly vanish.

Moving up the corridor, I pass a great number of open doors, through which waft various breakfast smells, borne upon streams of sunlight. In these anonymous rooms exist the spectres of the aged, the declined flesh, what I, too, will in time become. An old man, dressed in an impeccable shirt and tie and pressed navy pants, sits with his legs crossed before a breakfast tray, peering at the contents of a teacup, stirring sugar into it with a kind of otherworldly detachment. A woman with an astonishing braid of silver hair regards her small Bible with an air of resentment or thwarted expectation. The presence of this decay and dissolution comforts me. I imagine myself old, and Liam old, and Sam, but when I try to position my mother within this frame, I discover that her essential fabric is not pliable and will not be manipulated. There is a permanence about her that is achieved only with great difficulty or great stubbornness.

The United Church minister is a woman. This is the first thing that startles me; I would never have considered my mother progressive enough to allow another woman to officiate at her wedding. The regular minister needs prostate surgery, it seems, with an urgency that is always comical. As a result, his replacement — a tiny woman with tilted blue eyes that make her look like a demented fairy — has come to join my mother and my uncle in holy matrimony.

Liam has accompanied me, without requiring the kind of explanations that might make things awkward. I am wearing a dress. To venture thus into the outside world without the protection of my usual armour is discomfiting, but there is at least Liam.

When he comes to pick me up at my house, I am struck not only by how beautiful he looks, but by how I myself react to his beauty. I am flushed and dizzy, as though I were a teenaged girl on her first date. Liam is a handsome man, not overly tall but taller than me; his eyes are a shade of green I have never seen before, deep and moist; his narrow face is watchful and intellectual.

I admit that I have never looked at him as a man before. On the occasions when we have actually been together, it was always to talk about some aspect of my work, to pore over manuscript corrections or discuss subsidiary rights, marketing and promotion. He was a presence, speaking across the table, and that was all. Or else he was my protector at signings and launches, steering me away from danger.

When he reaches to unlock the car door, I catch the scent of his cologne, and it affects me like ether. It is just the sort of cologne that I wouldn't expect Liam to wear: it smells like the outdoors, the forest and the sea. I would have expected him to choose something that smelled like books, old libraries, manuscripts. I imagined he would smell like the Memorial University library stacks. Instead, the scent of him is magical and altogether fey, as if he had stepped out of the mist some morning and decided to remain.

"Are you all right with this, Stella?" I am hunched against the passenger door of his ancient Volvo, saying nothing, considering how strange my legs feel in pantyhose, how my toes seem to curl with resentment inside my polished leather boots.

"I'm fine." On the pretext of gazing through the windshield, I allow myself a long look at him from the corner of my eye. The journey from Topsail to Elsinore takes time, and I know we will have to make conversation of some sort. Besides the obvious topic of my books, I wonder what I can possibly talk to him about; it's not as if we have anything in common.

"You don't have to pretend it's making you happy. Sure, your father is hardly cold." He glances at me, his long fingers curled around the steering wheel with an easy grace.

"I know." I wish he'd stop talking about it. If I knew him better, I could say something, I could ask him to change the subject. But I know I won't — I'm too afraid of being impolite, so I will put up with it. I've always been that way. Fearing abandonment way beyond what is normal or acceptable, I have instead chosen the extreme opposite: separation and seclusion.

"You look pretty." His eyes crinkle at the corners as he smiles. "Or am I not supposed to say that?"

I wonder why he would say it in the first place, but I don't comment. I know he is Irish and therefore given to loquacious flattery; I know he can't possibly mean what he says. I am afraid that the drive to my mother's house will be the longest hours of my life, trapped in this rubbishy Volvo with Liam, acutely aware of how close his leg is to mine and how his hand may sometimes brush mine when he reaches across to shift gears. When he tilts his head to check the side mirror, I can see a fluttery pulse in his neck, just above his collar. He is more delicate than I realized.

After a while, he turns on the radio: classical music, someone sawing industriously at a cello or a violin, coaxing smooth, buttery tones from it like teasing a cat. In allowing the music to wash over me and soothe me, I give myself permission to relax, and I feel somewhat guilty. Liam is beating time on his leg with the fingers of his right hand while his left hand holds the wheel. The sky outside the car is fretful, mauzy; the road is damp. It is the day after the first of the year.

She will be married in that blue dress, I know it. It has some kind of totemic power for her, it embodies all the things she wishes for herself and can no longer have. The dress is what came before I did.

I remember when I was a teenager, when my mother and I had made some kind of uneasy truce, she would take me into her closet as into a *sanctum sanctorum* and show the dress to me, hidden under layers of black garbage bags, protected from the light, the elements, the air itself. It became an icon, a testament to the enduring power of self-delusion, and she would tell me stories about it, stories that became more vivid and cruel with each telling, stories that inevitably cast her in the role of a dewy-eyed debutante, an outport belle. All the boys vied with each other to be the first to dance with Mim Bristow; Mim Bristow was the prettiest girl in the school. I know this particular fact to be true because I have seen photos of my mother as a young woman, and she was indeed beautiful — more beautiful than I could ever be — but hard, as though crusted over, lacquered.

I tried to touch the dress once, overcome with reverence, but she slapped my hand away before my fingers could make contact. *Don't you be putting your dirty paws on it,* she hissed at me, her eyes flashing like an angry cat's. *I haven't kept it all these years for you to go mucking it up.* I remember I cried — I couldn't have been more than twelve or thirteen — and she gathered me awkwardly into her arms, as if she'd seen someone on television do this and figured it was correct behaviour in this situation. I held myself absolutely still as she rocked and crooned, afraid that if I moved the spell would be broken. The scent of her flesh I seemed to remember dimly, a memory cached in the secret chambers of my soul, a cloying, womanish smell like clotted talcum powder or dried milk. She patted the same spot on my back over and over, thumping so that the blows echoed off my ribcage, enraptured with her own remorse: *mea culpa, mea maxima culpa.* I knew that whenever I saw the dress from now on, it would hold a sound for me, the hollow clapping of her palm against my spine as she inexpertly sounded my depth.

There is a little snow in the yard when we pull up; someone has come out with a shovel and tidied it to each side of the walkway. I know it was Uncle Joss because my mother wouldn't know which end of a shovel to wield, having never touched one in her life. I am astonished by the mathematical precision of the shovelling. He has carefully peeled back the layer of snow as far as the gravel underneath, the crushed sea shells and rounded beach rocks; the sea might wash up to the door and my mother would never hear it.

Liam waits until I have let myself out of the car, standing quietly by my side and shivering as his overcoat flaps open in the cold wind. Instinctively, I clutch a handful of his lapel and yank him toward me, button the coat with a decisive pat. I raise my eyes and he is gazing down at me; his scrutiny is so intense it makes me uneasy, like being spied upon by the Good Folk, some modern remnant of the Daone Sidhe. I expect he intends to say something, but he is quiet, and after a moment we go into the house.

The kitchen and the living room look as though a bomb has gone off, but not just any bomb, a bomb made out of crepe paper, balloons and glitter, which has somehow contrived to burst and run down my mother's walls in an effect that borrows heavily from Jackson Pollock. I feel Liam's surprise, but he is too polite to say anything. Uncle Joss is in the kitchen, standing by the hot water boiler with a glass in his hand; clean shaven and dressed in what is obviously a new suit, he looks almost handsome. I realize that his eyes are kind, that it is impossible to hate him. When he moves to shake hands with Liam, his cherubic face splits in a grin. "You must be Stella's boyfriend, then."

Liam graciously accepts the glass of whisky that my uncle gives him and smiles wryly. "Well now, sir, I've tried a dozen times to make her love me, so I have, and I've had no luck with it at all." He inclines his head toward me. "I'm Stella's editor, Mr. Goulding." What might have been an awkward moment is successfully aborted by my uncle's good sense and Liam's good manners. I allow myself to hope a little.

My mother is wearing the dress.

I've been that nervous, look, I never thought I'd get in this dress, but I did. I think it's the smokes that does it — sure, I never feels like eating. All I minds is the smokes. I shouldn't be at the fags, I know, because that's what killed poor old Father, but it's really good on me nerves.

It fits the same as it always did. My God, I can't fool meself into thinking I'm fourteen again, but I don't look too bad, I must say. Don't say I wasn't nervous, I never slept a wink all last night. Joss stayed up to Marion's, just so we'd keep with the tradition. I tossed and turned all night, and round about four o'clock the smorning I finally got up out of it, went and made some coffee and had a fag. It was as cold as Hell's bells in the kitchen, so I had to light the fire, and I found meself thinking about my mother. I doubt she'll be at the house tomorrow, I said to meself. Not unless she comes out with Stella. I daresay Stella'll be there with that Irish fella, what's his name, Declan or Stephen or Eamonn or something. If she wasn't so queer in the head, sure, he might marry her. But Stella won't be married, I knows that for sure and certain. She's too contrary for any man to put up with her, and you knows what they says about the Irish men: all they wants is youngsters and the bottle, and not always in that order. I daresay if she married him he'd have her carted off to Armagh or Skibbereen or wherever, and she'd be up to her arse in youngsters before you could say Jack Robinson. I knows what the Irish is like. I'm some glad Joss isn't Irish — his great-grandar probably come over on the same boat from Devon as mine.

I wish the minister would hurry up. I haven't seen Joss yet, he's out in the kitchen, probably dipping into the booze already. To tell you the truth, I don't know what I bought it for, it's not like Stella ever takes a drop. Of course, that Irish fella might like some. He'll probably take a drink or two.

I wonders about the dead sometimes, whether they can see the living, and if they knows what's going on with us, like. I thinks about me grandmother up to the cemetery. She's been buried these forty years or more, up there alongside the rest of 'em. I guess if she can see everything, then Jack can, too. I wonder what he thinks of it all. I suppose it's not that much of a surprise to en. Or maybe it is. I don't know no more.

She is wearing the dress. I knew she would wear the dress, but I have to give my mother credit: it fits her like a second skin, as if she were still sixteen and as lithe and girlish as she was before I came.

She's bought some kind of little turquoise hat with a veil, and I find this appropriately demure on her part, this impulse to partially hide the face, as if she were in purdah. It is inevitable that she will no longer mourn my father, seeing as how she is to be joined now to my uncle, but I must congratulate her, for she has brazened out her deception with a grace I have never seen in her before. Still, her appearance is unsettling, dizzying to me; it has the flavour of a partially remembered dream, one with all the conscious fringes of it cut off like a savaged pair of drapes. She is Mim Bristow, sixteen again and glowing like a fresh-cut rose. She is my grandmother, stepping off the boat from Britain. She is me.

I find myself clinging to Liam's arm as tightly as if I were standing on the deck of a schooner, full out in a heavy gale. I think about the walkway leading up to the house, crowded with crushed seashells and rounded beach rocks. Who will tell my mother when the ocean rushes to her door?

There is a supper afterwards, after the minister has gone, bearing with her the envelope my uncle gives her, hidden somewhere underneath her robes. On the outside landing, the wind catches her surplice, bellies it gloriously, then she plunges down into the trough, carried to her car as if on the sliding congress of a wave.

I am nauseous, and I beg off for a moment, find the door and go round the side of the house, leaving my mother and her high school dress inside the kitchen. My fingers find the roughness of the clapboard pleasing; here and there, tiny curls of paint that have sloughed themselves off from the house cling to my fingers like eyelashes, penitent and white. I crouch against the wall, turn my face full into the freezing January wind, inhale it as if it were the breath of life.

"She's an odd old bird, so she is." Liam peers around the corner of the house, his hair whipped about his head like a dusky halo. "Am I bothering you?"

He is most definitely bothering me because I need to be alone now, but I am polite, and I cannot bear to drive him away, today of all days, when he is such a rock for me. "Of course not."

"This was kind of quick, wasn't it?" He peers at me with a sympathy that I am altogether uncomfortable with. "Your mother, I mean."

All of a sudden, I really don't care what my mother does. Or else I do and am trying to pretend otherwise. "She does things like that. On a whim." I don't want to talk about her, so I push away from the peeling wall and start walking, ascending the small hill behind the house. The house is on a point, with sea front and back. There is a pebble beach there where I used to play when I was a child, poking at things with sticks and catching congers and harassing the poor demented squid that were often trapped in tidal pools. I remember Nanny Bristow telling me tales of the selkies, cast out of Heaven by the Lord and made to live as men on land and seals in the sea, and I used to wait by the water's edge for them. I cannot remember when I stopped waiting, when I stopped expecting that something miraculous would happen to me, but I did, I must have, because I no longer believe in things like this. The numinous has no hold over me.

"This reminds me of where I used to play when I was a boy." Liam is a steady presence beside me, his hands shoved into his pockets against the cold. "Jesus, that's a chilly wind."

"You had a beach like this in Armagh?" I can see the foamy tops of the waves, far out. If I squint and strain the muscles of my face, I can imagine that my father is out there, plying the water with his nets, dragging drowned sailors from the ocean floor, *My Nancy-O*. Sometimes he would let me burst the waterpups that had formed upon his wrists.

"Not in Armagh." Liam is squinting, too, and I wonder if he is seeing anything or if he is just protecting himself against the wind. "Near Barcelona, where I used to stay in the summer with my aunt."

I often imagine him as that little boy, sitting on a sun-washed Catalonian beach, eating oranges and squinting into the sky. "I've never been anywhere." This is the truth. There is nowhere I particularly want to go. Even being here in Elsinore again, trapped in my mother's poisonous sphere like an insect under glass, I have no real desire to flee. Things will inevitably go forward as they always do, whether or not I participate. Life does not require my participation, and it is just as well that I absent myself from all proceedings whenever possible.

He tells me about his aunt's house and how every year he would return to that same beach and sit there on the sand, eating the same oranges or variations, and waiting for something.

"What were you waiting for?" I ask.

"My grandmother used to tell us stories when we were little . . . about the Roane, the selkies." He takes my arm and leads me back towards the house, the cold wind clawing at our faces, our exposed hands. "I thought that if I waited there and was a very good boy, I might see one." He laughs, and there is something at once child-like and awkward in his laughter, and I feel myself suffused with a dangerous gratitude.

My mother and Uncle Joss sit at opposite ends of the table like the more obscure members of the Royal Family, and my mother carves the chicken with admirable precision. She has removed her tiny turquoise hat, and her head emerges from the rolled neckline of her dress, large and vaguely frightening. I wonder if this is where the human species first learns fear, subjected to the huge maternal head leering out of the darkness over the bassinet. It is the subject matter for a thousand ill-conceived reconstructions: jack-o-lanterns, party masks, the nastier type of doll. My mother extends her hand to Liam — "See the ring he give me?" — but not to me, and I am forced to examine the thin gold band from a safe distance.

I cannot wait for it to be over, and then it is over, and I am stepping into the Volvo with Liam, extending my cheek to Uncle Joss, waving with feigned cheerfulness at my mother.

Some miles out on the Trans-Canada Highway, I have to ask Liam to pull over. In the semidarkness of the winter evening, I lean out and vomit without provocation, bringing up everything my mother fed me. Liam reaches to pat my back, but I warn him off with guttural noises; this type of purge must always occur in an attitude of absolute abjection, the mystic approaching the Throne of Grace.

"Perhaps you should've stayed in town." We are drawing closer to the inhabited strip of the Avalon, and there is an eerie orange glow on the horizon. Liam's face is lit from beneath by the dashboard lights, his nose and chin mere pale projections. "You don't have to —"

"Yes, I do." How to explain it to him? If I did not go, my mother would kill me — would find a way to kill me. A poisoned letter in an envelope dusted with arsenic, curare in the raisin buns, a blow dart puffed through my kitchen window. She is that powerful, I know. She must be appeased, she is capable of doing monstrous harm, of wreaking mad and horrible destruction.

It begins to snow, great pelting flakes that yield to a driving wind, so that we are moving inside a revolving funnel of white. Liam turns the wipers on and then the radio, drowning out my thoughts with the dissonance of Bartok.

Once when I was little I got trapped inside the lighthouse at Elsinore in the middle of a blizzard. Although there was only one window in that great tube of stone, I did not feel suffocated by my isolation, my lack of sight. When my father came and found me, I was disappointed.

CHAPTER EIGHT

It is somewhere near the middle of February, or perhaps past it, I'm not sure. It is freezing cold outside, the kind of bitter chill that sinks into the bones; I am sitting at my kitchen table, overlooking the frozen landscape of my back yard, pretending to correct my book galleys when in fact I am contemplating the sad fact of the February trees.

The weeks have disappeared behind me, like the waters of a fast-rushing stream; I have lain for what feels like years in a kind of stupor, a gluttony of rest. I have pills that make me sleep, that bring oblivion for as long as I want it, as long as I need it. I am careful always to keep a good supply of them on hand because such blessed insensibility is hard to come by. I am like an eighteenth-century hysteric, the contemplative with her laudanum.

My mother and Uncle Joss have been married for six weeks, or just about. Since the day of her wedding, I have not heard from her, and I believe it is better this way. I need to divorce myself from her, mask my feelings, make sure she can never discern them. She is capable of great destruction.

The day after the wedding, I made myself sit down with pen and paper and write a letter to Sam. It was necessary to explain the naked facts, and he is a suitable repository for my attempts at confession. I think it is because he is so far away and poses no threat; I can spill my guts to him and not think twice about it. I wrote the whole story to him, from beginning to end, leaving out Liam, of course.

Today is a good day to stay inside and work; correcting galleys is a job that I particularly like. Mundane and yet demanding, it leaves no room for reflection and the other habits of an uneasy mind. Red pen in hand, cup of coffee at my elbow, I can be content; this is as close to myself as I ever get.

I went for a walk this morning, very early, just as daylight was slicing open the horizon. The air was heavy with the damp chill that heralds weather; the weatherman says it will snow today, and I believe him. In February the weather is capricious.

My pathway has been free of litter for some months, ever since the winter came on. Even though there has been precious little snow (and that soon washed away by rain), they have not come back, they have not invaded this place, and I feel a strange gratitude toward them. I can walk a fair distance through this way before my path joins with a public walking trail and doubles back upon itself, venturing into common terrain where I might be encountered, spied upon, marked. The pleasure lies in being absolutely alone, or fostering that illusion in any case: were I to meet another person on my path, my faith in this place would be shattered.

I have not heard much from Liam since my mother's wedding. I expect it's because he's busy. This is a hectic time of year for him, and I've heard (perhaps he mentioned it in passing) that his father is unwell and wants to go back to Ireland. Maybe Liam is there now, in Armagh, honouring his father's request to take him back, recover for him the essence of that spot where his hope died, outside their tidy house. I'm not worried about Liam. Liam always knows what to do.

There is mail for me, mail that has been sitting on the floor inside my front porch for ages. At some time in my period of oblivion, it must have fallen through the mail slot, but I don't remember hearing it. Most of it is rubbish, of course, but there is a letter from

Sam, about two weeks old. There is a second letter, a letter from my mother.

I don't know how long it's been here, or what a letter like this means. My mother isn't in the habit of writing me letters. On the odd occasion when she feels somewhat charitable towards me, she will enclose two or three handwritten recipes in an envelope and forward them to me with a note: *This is good with cinnamon on it.* Sometimes there is a brief news report, bits of gossip about the few remaining denizens of Elsinore, but other than that, she does not write me letters.

I know this can be nothing good. Curiously, I am not afraid of it, and when I move to open it, my fingers are only trembling a little bit. I pretend that this is a good sign — that I have conquered my fear, that I have effectively broken the hold she has over me.

I hates having to write a letter like this, but the time is come for you to be told the truth.

I hates having to write a letter like this, but God knows, I got to tell her the truth. Jack has been dead these three months, and I figures I got to try and tell her sometime, so she knows. I can't tell her to her face, and I'm no good at talking on the phone. It's not something I'd ever say to her in person, anyway — I don't think she'd appreciate that at all.

My Jesus, how am I going to say the like of this? I suppose the best way is to just come right out and say it, for God's sake. Me hand is shaking that hard, look, I can hardly hold the pen.

I haven't been feeling too well the past couple of months, ever since Joss and I got married. I'm too old for it to be nerves, so I think perhaps me blood is down. What I needs is a tonic. I hates going to the doctor, the way they pokes and prods at ye, but if I'm not cleared up by the spring, I suppose I should go. I'm awful tired all the time, but that might just be me age. I'm coming up to the menopause now, too, I knows it. I'll be fifty-three my birthday: the same age my mother was when she went on the change of life. I feels right tired all the time, hot and cold, like I could sleep the clock round if I'd a mind to.

Joss and I gets along pretty good, though, and at least he's here, not like Jack. Of course, he's a man, and he's like they all are as far as that goes, but he got nice manners. That's Marion's doing — she always was right hoity-toity, Eleanor too. I swear that's why Eleanor went off the deep end.

My Jesus . . . I minds when I was about nine . . . Lord God, I haven't thought about this in years, not since before Stella was born . . . yes, I was about nine. Our old house used to sit right up agin the beach, with the back of 'er right tight to the water almost, the way my father built it. My mother used to say that if there was ever a tidal wave, sure, we'd all be swept out to sea, but my father told her never to mind, we'd just put a few floats on 'er and move 'er somewhere else, like people done.

I had a bad cold one time in the fall, right around Halloween, it was, and I got up out of bed this night to go and get a drink of water out of the bucket in the back pantry — we never had running water in the house then, so my father used to bring it from the well and put a bucket in the back pantry. If you wanted a drink, you could take the lid off the bucket and dip up what you wanted with the dipper.

I went down this night to get a drink, my God, I was burning up with the fever. It was a real frosty cold night, and everything outdoors was white with the hoarfrost. The floor in the back pantry was just boards put down, and it was that cold against my bare feet that it felt like it was burning me. If I stood up on me tiptoes I could see out the window, could see all the way down to the water. It was a clear night, too, with the moon out, and that made it even better. Everything was right silvery, it was some pretty.

I seen the woman down by the water, and I figured I was having the Old Hag or something. I had to blink me eyes a half-dozen times to make sure I wasn't dreaming, but she was there, wearing a long white dress or a nightgown, with her hair down around her shoulders, right black and wavy, like my hair was when I was younger. She was stood on the beach, staring into the water like she was looking for something or waiting for something, waving her hands back and forth like someone doing a spell.

I must've stood there and watched her for ages, so help me God, because the next thing I knew, my father was there behind me, hauling on his boots, and I heard en cursing, *Lord liftin' Jesus Christ that woman, that friggin' woman.* He seen me standing there and bawled out at me, "Git back to bed! This is none of your business!"

He ran down and caught her under the arms and tried to lift her up, but she buckled her knees and crouched down on the ground. I seen en pointing out to the water and shouting something, waving his arms like he was really mad. He had on a pair of green work pants like he wore to go fishing, and his logans and a workshirt not done up right because he was in a hurry. He grabbed her by the hand and started hauling her along the ground, so she fell over on her knees, then tumbled onto her side, all scrunched up. I didn't want to look at it, but I couldn't stop looking at it, and then he picked her up — picked my mother up — by the scruff of the neck like you'd pick up a kitten. He hove her over his shoulder and came on up toward the house, holding onto her. If I closes me eyes, I can see it now so clear as the day.

I don't know what she was doing down by the water like that, unless she was trying to do away with herself. With my mother, you never know.

I hates having to write a letter like this. I wonder why I don't believe her when she says such things. I imagine her crouched over her kitchen table in Elsinore, writing with the pen clenched between her fingers, her eyes gleaming with something very like glee. She would doubtless have convinced herself that it was her moral duty to write such a document, like other people write epitaphs. Perhaps she could hardly restrain herself from blurting it out at their wedding, standing in the kitchen.

Uncle Joss is not your uncle. He's your father.

The words blur before my eyes, like a shape seen at a distance; even holding the paper at arm's length, I still am unable to see the sentence clearly. If I blink, it might change dimensions of its own accord, transform into something that I am more able to accept. I am not upset, I am unable to be upset just yet, I will doubtless get upset later, once this bizarre revelation has had time to sink into my brain, create a home for itself, move around and get comfortable.

I go to put the kettle on, gazing at myself in the mirror over the sink; in this uncertain light, it seems as if my eyes are blue like his, like Uncle Joss's. Or perhaps they are no colour at all. What if, in later years, I came to resemble my mother? I don't believe I could stand it.

So this is what she has been bursting to tell me, then: that the father I so lovingly buried isn't my father at all, but my uncle; the uncle that my mother married isn't my uncle but my father, already her husband by right of shared procreation. I ought to be surprised, but all I feel is a cold thrill, like biting on a piece of wood.

The other letter is from Sam. The handwriting is crabbed and shaky, slanting off the pale blue envelope and disappearing into nothing. His handwriting has never looked like this, as if he'd signed his name in the dark. I remember that in eight weeks, give or take, he will be in Halifax, doing his film. I remember that he expects me to join him there, to meet him as one would meet a friend or confidante.

The letter is crammed onto two sheets of paper, every possible space filled with a tiny, crabbed writing that I can barely recognise as Sam's. Something about this frightens me, but I'm not sure why — could it be some sort of warning, a warning to which I must pay heed? And if so, a warning of what?

He is highly emotional — he's an actor — but I haven't ever seen anything like this. He's in some sort of crisis, I know it, and there's nothing I can do, so far away from him. He goes through these passages — "phases" as he calls them — when he is either depressed or manic. He's supposed to take medicines for the condition, but he won't, he claims it dampens his artistry to the point where he can no longer function as an actor. I think he avoids the drugs because they make him what he fears the most: merely ordinary.

One night, over the phone, he told me all about his life. It was very late, or perhaps very early in the morning, and it was summer, which meant that I had given myself liberty to leave the windows and the doors open. A huge moth had wandered into the foyer, and it flittered round the light fixture, its wings making a soft, plushy sound against the glass, like someone slapping velvet. I was sitting in the big leather chair near the sliding glass doors that let into my backyard, listening to the night sounds.

Sam's mother's name was Dora, and she had a younger husband, an Italian with the penetrating, oddly lifeless eyes of garden statuary. Sam was always afraid of his stepfather but never knew why, and since his father died when he was very young, he had no suitable object around which to frame his longing for male closeness. He always wondered, he told me, what his life would have been like had his father lived long enough to know him, to really know him. He told me all these things in his crisp, almost accentless voice, never lingering over anything of note but delivering all to me as one might hand off a parcel of dirty shirts.

He told me about being at a boarding school, a brutal place, an Elizabethan fortress located some miles from London, where the older boys made a practice of holding his head in the toilet and flushing or beating him round the shins with an electric cord until his skin broke open and bled. The boarding school became necessary after his mother married the Italian because she and her new husband wanted to travel and spent much of the year abroad. His mother told him this arrangement would be eminently more fair to him and would allow her time to know his stepfather as she ought. Without Sam's saying very much, he gave me to understand that he had always resented his mother for this, even as everything within him strained towards her, eager for the love he knew she kept somewhere but would never relinquish to him. "She's the most beautiful woman I've ever seen." He seemed very wistful as he said this, as if her beauty were somehow his fault and a grievous failing of them both.

In the letter, he is talking about Scotland, about how he wants to go to Scotland to visit his grandfather, whom he calls Grandar. There is something wrong, I know, because he is supposed to come to Canada in April, and I am wondering if he has forgotten all of it, forgotten even about visiting me.

I should do something to help him, but this is impossible. I am unable to help anyone, and certainly there is no effective help I could give anyway. I think about my mother and my Uncle Joss in the house at Elsinore, framed by the living room window, sitting together and watching television. I cannot understand how she could have waited all these years to tell me the most essential truth of my existence.

She must have got the letter by now, so I daresay she knows. She haven't phoned me or nothing, though. Not like she would phone me. The last time we talked was when Joss and I got married, just after New Year.

Jack was away a lot when we was first married, and when Stella was born, it was even worse. I don't know, it was like he couldn't stand to be around the house. It was like he had to always be out on the water, always at the fish, and if he wasn't out on the water, he was down to the rooms, salting down the fish or knitting up twine. He only come home to eat and go to bed, now, and that's the truth. It turns my stomach to be talking about it. He was never a good husband to me.

I minds the warm evenings in July and August, when Stella was a baby, and I used to take her down to the slipway and wait for Jack's boat to come in. "Do you want a bit of supper?" I'd ask en, and he'd always say, "Yes, maid," or something like that, and then come home and haive his fishy old clothes down on the kitchen floor. "Come here, maid," he'd say, grabbing after me. "I haven't seen ye all day." Like I was going to let the like of that touch me with his filthy paws, and him smelling like fish, and Stella, then, tissing and screeching in the cot over by the window.

I was in the bathtub last night and I noticed that I got some kind of a pimple coming out on one of me breasts, over on the left one, it is. Sort of sunk in like a dimple, and red around it. It don't hurt, though, so I don't know if it's anything serious or not. I suppose I should go to the doctor, but I'm frightened to death it's cancer. Eva died of cancer, and I don't want to have it, they says it runs in families. No one in our family ever had it, so it can't be anything bad. Sure, I'm not that old, not like Rita Tizzard was when she died. She was always the floor lady over to the fish plant. I remember that summer I worked there, when Stella was small, and Rita was in charge of the night shift. My God, didn't she drive us some hard. She used to stand over me when I went to wash me pans to make sure I done it the way she wanted it. And I minds one time she took this jesus big pair of shears and chopped off Leona Button's long fingernails. Didn't Leona bawl, my God, you'd think Rita had chopped off her fingers. Of course, Rita was always as hard as nails. She didn't care, my dear, for chick nor child. She was that hard, I heard she smacked one missus in the face up on the cooking floor. They were at the fish one night, this was in the summer, cooking it to package it up later on for the deep-fried fish boxes, that stuff that goes to the supermarket. Missus — I think it was young Rhoda Tucker — said something about Rita behind her back as Rita went walking by, and by the Lord dyin', if she didn't whip around and smack her a good one in the mouth. We were always half afraid of Rita. When she got the cancer in her breast, then, it was right over her heart, right on the left side. They went and took her breast off, but it was too late. Once it gets exposed to the air, that's it. It went into her brain, and she was never herself after that. Poor old soul, even though none of us liked her. We all thought she was too crooked to die, sure. She did, though.

Stella must've got that letter by now. I wonder if she read it, I wonder what she thinks. I suppose I should of sot down with her, me and Joss, and told her together, like. Perhaps I could of got Joss to tell her, but men is no good at that sort of thing.

I wish Stella was married. I wish she had someone. Even that Irish fellow, Stephen or Eamonn or Declan, whatever his name is. He might be all right. He'd be some company for her, sure.

I've been thinking about Jack a lot lately, too. I never lets on to Joss anything about it — what he don't know won't hurt en — but I do. I thinks about Jack a lot. He owned land before we were married, land that his father had, that his grandfather and great-grandfather owned, land that they had way back when they all come over on the boat. When his father died, Jack got the land, see, him being the oldest son. Joss was the youngest and he got whatever was left over: the house, a few tools belonging to the old man, things like that. The two girls was in between Jack and Joss, although I think Marion is older than Eleanor.

Eleanor always hated my guts. I minds when me and Jack first started going out together, we used to be up to his house on Saturday nights to watch the wrestling. My God, the wrestling was always a big draw in them days. You'd get five or six or eight of the men crowded into the front room to look at the television.

Jack's father was old, even then. Him and missus got married when they were really too old to be at it, but of course I knows now, the nature of the beast and whatnot. The men got to be hitched up to a woman or else they don't know what to do with theirselves. They ends up like poor old Skipper Duncan, over to the lighthouse, playing with himself and watching the boats come in.

Eleanor looked after the old man after his mind was gone. He was wearing diapers and everything then, poor old soul. He used to like to sit at the table in the kitchen and look out the window, and he'd keep calling for his dead wife, Bride: "Is that you, Bridie? Come over till I sees ye." He used to talk old foolishness sometimes, about being out after the seals and that, and then he'd get all upset and start bawling, and Eleanor used to have to calm him down. Poor old soul, never had a tooth in his head, she used to have to mash up a bit of bread in a saucer of milk for en, like you'd give a baby. I suppose now, Eleanor thought that when he died she'd get the whole works of it: the house, the land, the boat the old man had, all the gear. Although what in the name of God Eleanor was going at with the gear and the boat is beyond my ken. Anyhow, that's not how it works around here. It's the men that got the rights to stuff like that. Sure, she was probably going to get married and go off somewhere, anyway. She was always going on about how she was getting out of Elsinore: *I hates this place. As soon as I can, I'm getting out of here*. She was always saying that, like Elsinore wasn't good enough for her, like she couldn't stand to be here. Oh, didn't that burn me, listening to the like of that, and my God, once she got started you couldn't shut her up. She'd go on and on. Jack said she used to have her tongue hinged in the middle so it could flap at both ends. Yes, she was going to move in to St. John's and have a career — the way she said it used to turn my stomach, like she was going to discover the cure for cancer. She always wanted to be like a man, sure. I never understood the like of that, why she wanted to have that land and all the rest of it. What did she think was going to happen? I don't know how any woman wants to play a man's part in the world. It's pretty bad when a man got to step aside, now, and let a girl take over. It's not natural.

I remember when Jack asked me to marry en, and we went up to the house to show everyone the ring he got for me that he ordered out of the Eaton's catalogue and had come from Toronto. She was looking at that, my dear, like her eyes were going to start right out of her head, and that's the truth. And she always talked right proper, like she was better than anyone else. She was sent away to be taught by the nuns in St. John's when she was about seven or eight. The old woman, God rest her soul, was a Catholic, and even though Jack's father was Salvation Army, she wanted the girls to have a good education. Sure, Eleanor took her nursing in to the Grace and worked in St. John's for a couple years. The old man got sick, then, with the diabetes, and they thought he was going to go right quick, but he never. Eleanor had to give up her nursing and come home out of it, because her mother was dead by then, and there was no one to look after the old man. Marion couldn't do it all by herself, sure. Eleanor even had an apartment in on New Gower Street, her and two other nurses, but she had to come back and look after the old man.

Nobody ever leaves Elsinore. You're born here, you marries here, and you dies here. Eleanor was always too big for her boots. This place was good enough for me, and it should have been good enough for her.

I wonder if that's where Stella gets it to. Maybe Stella is like Eleanor. They say it gets carried down in the blood, things like that. Maybe that's why she's the way she is. She was always high-strung, I used to try and talk to her when she was younger, and sure you couldn't talk sensible to her. She'd start bawling all the time. She was right soft-hearted, and it used to drive me nuts. She'd talk to my mother, but she'd never say anything to me. At least she'd talk to my mother, mind you, she might never have said a word to anyone, that's the way Stella always was. She'd keep everything inside of her and write stories about it. That's what she does now, writes stories about everything, about us, about her father and me. I knows she does it. I knows she's writing things like that, running us down. She'll be sorry for it one of these days, when I'm dead and gone.

I remember Eleanor telling old Mr. Goulding one time how she didn't want me to have Jack. I was out in the front room and she was in one of the back bedrooms, changing the old fellow's diaper for en. "She's not suited to our Jack," she said, like someone in one of them fancy novels. "I don't see why you don't put a stop to it." She always talked right proper, like she had all these words in the back of her mouth and was frightened to death she'd drop too many at once. She never talked the way everyone else did. The way she talked, you'd think the Queen was visiting. And then coming out of the bedroom and seeing me there and smiling an evil little smile, like a cat that just eat a bird. Didn't that make me sick. I wanted to smack the mouth off of her, that's what I did.

She never wanted me to marry Jack. None of that crowd did. But I got en after all. For all the good it done me.

I've lots of time to think these days. Sometimes I can sit here by the window and look out at the birds and feel like I'm home again. It's not like home, but that's the way my memories are.

I had the dream about going to Skye again last night, Mother and me and Nell, and Father with his tweed jacket and his pipe. It was winter this time, and everything was misty, and I could hear Nell calling to me in the mist, but we were young again, and Cousin Albert was there, and his sister Margaret. The boat that we were on, it moved along the water with no oars, no engine, a magical boat. When I first woke up, I heard my father calling to me out of the mist, and we all but bumped the shore before the nurse woke me: "Time for your pills, Mrs. Bristow." That red-haired lassie with the bandy legs, the one that reminds me of Judy's wee sister Kathleen. Kathleen married an Irishman from Armagh; his father was in the IRA. I remember that. I remember my father telling us about it, the Orange and the Green.

Mim's gone and gotten married again. Well, my God, it doesn't surprise me any. She never had a brain in her head. I often wonder where I went wrong with her. I never thought she'd turn out the way she did.

I remember when she was going with Jack Goulding and she got into it with Eleanor. Eleanor always had a tongue on her and always fancied herself, and her father nothing but an illiterate fisherman. Mim came home one night, bawling about how Eleanor said something to her, and I warned her. I told her she should know better. I didn't raise her to be cheap like that. She went into the bedroom and tore her face up — tore her face up with her fingernails till it was all bloody and I had to take her to Doctor Snook to get it looked at.

Of course, she had to get married to Jack. It's not what they do nowadays, but it's what we did back then. I didn't want her to get married. Not that I had anything against the lad, but I didn't raise Mim to go and do what she did. I told her I'd send her to the nursing school in St. John's, or she could go live with Nell and take her university in England with my mother's people.

She wouldn't listen, though. She always was headstrong. Like my crowd, I must admit. I remember when I met Ted during the war. My poor old mother begged me not to marry him, but I did. It just about broke her heart, I know. I suppose the young people have to go their own way, regardless.

CHAPTER NINE

I suppose I got to go to the doctor. That pimple I got, I had another look at it last night, and it's not going away. I put some ointment on it, but it never done nothing. It's still there, like a hole, only it's red inside. Yes, I got to go.

I never heard nothing from Stella about the letter I sent her. She won't say nothing to me now until she sees me again. That's all I needs, her ranting and raving at me. Lord Jesus, sure she's half cracked anyway. "I think I'll go to the doctor," I told Joss. He was sitting down to the table having a cup of tea and a raisin bun. He was getting ready to go to bed, listening to the news on VOCM before he went in to the bedroom. Joss don't hold with having a radio in the bedroom, he says he can't get to sleep with that blasting and blaring away. "Sure, you haven't got to have it on if you're trying to sleep," I told en. But he don't listen to nothing. He's just like Jack was. Jack never listened to nothing I told en, sure. I minds how it was when I wanted to get married to Jack. This was after Eleanor went mental with the old man up to the house, told en I wasn't fit to be married to Jack and all that. You knows what men are like, too, you got to step right in and put your foot down or else they'll take their arse in their hand and run away. Jack was always that type, would never go agin his sister or the old man.

I went out for a walk one night, down to the beach. I used to like to go down there, looking for winkles. Sometimes me and Eva would get a few mussels and boil 'em in a tin can on the bonfire. I can taste 'em in me mouth, just thinking about it. I loves a good feed of mussels. Sure, the ones you gets now, you can hardly eat, they're all poisoned with the acid rain and all that. I wouldn't put 'em in me mouth.

Joss was down on the beach that night, stood up by the water flicking rocks. He wasn't so stout then as he is now, and he was a nice-looking fellow. Eleanor said Joss would never get anywhere. She told the old man that if anyone was going to make something of hisself, it'd be Jack. Of course, that was all foolishness because Jack couldn't even read or write. At least Joss got his grade eleven, and he done something with hisself, took that old car he bought off of Headley and made it into a taxi. He made good money, too, taking the crowd back and forth to St. John's or over to Bonavista. One brother is just as good as the other, that's what I always said. Joss was just as good as Jack. "What's ye doing?" I had on me new twin set that Aunt Dorothy sent from overseas and the skirt that Eva's poor old mother made up for me on the sewing machine. I looked some nice. "Haiving rocks out there, is ye? Sure, you'll fill up the water with all that."

He never said nothing. I think he figured out what I was on about. I think he knew why I come down there in the first place. He knew Jack was out at the fish with Headley. He knew what I wanted. I never had no underpants on. I never put none on because they were all washed out, and I had none clean. I opened up me legs for him and lied down on the sand. It was right warm on the beach — this was in the summer. Right warm, the sand was, just like skin. Of course, Joss was just like all the men, right quick at it, hammering into me and then giving out with this big grunt at the end.

Jack and I never done it like that. It was right nice, like being in church sometimes. I remember Jack and I went to the lighthouse one night when we were courting, and we got a bit carried away, and I let him put it inside me, but he pulled back before he could come and shot it out on the ground instead. He put his fingers in me, then, so I could see what it felt like, and it felt some good. It wasn't too long before I knew I was going to have a baby. I never needed anyone to tell me, either. Eva and I got the book and looked it up, and I knew what was going to happen. I went up to Jack's house one night after supper. Eleanor was at the sink washing dishes, and old Mr. Goulding was sitting by the window, half asleep. I went right up to Jack at the supper table where he was smoking his pipe and I told en: "It's all over with now. You got to marry me."

Eleanor had this dish in her hand, some kind of big plate with roses all around the edges of it. She dropped that on the floor with a crash and started screaming and bawling. She run over and latched on to old Mr. Goulding, screeching out like she was burned. "You can't let her into the family, Dad. She'll take every blessed thing we got." Joss had to come and take her out of the room, and I heard her bawling all the way up the stairs.

Jack used to go off to the fish for ages and ages when Stella was small, leave me there all alone with the youngster, and her staring at me with her great big eyes all day long. When she got older, I used to put her outside in the yard while I was doing me work and lock the door after her. I used to say to her, "Don't come back till it's suppertime." It was the only bit of peace I ever got. The men are all alike, sure. It's the same thing with Joss, even now. I only married en so I wouldn't have to be by meself when I gets old. I can't face that, ending up like Eleanor, up there in that big old house all by herself after the old man died. It was never no comfort when Jack was alive. He was always gone to the fish, sometimes for as long as three months if he was up the Labrador. Even when he was home, sure, he never paid me no mind, he'd be across the road in the rooms or up to the post office, talking to Headley and them, talking about nothing. Or else he'd be out to the store, sitting on the big wooden barrel that Ches Fifield had the Purity biscuits in, eating a slice of bologna and drinking a bottle of Coke and talking to Pat O'Brien. He never said nothing to me, only asked me how I was and if he had either clean shirt to wear to the Salvation Army on a Sunday. Sure, Stella never looked nothing like him, and he never once asked me about it.

When Stella was a youngster, I used to get woke up at night with the cramps in me legs. I had awful bad cramps like that for years, until the doctor figured out it was the varicose veins, and by and by, she'd come into the bedroom with some old foolishness about how she dreamed about whales. It put me in mind of this dream I used to have all the time when I was a young girl about two killer whales that beached theirselves one time, down where Joss got me with Stella. I used to dream how I was walking along the beach, and I'd see the two of 'em there, singing like whales does, and I used to try and pry underneath 'em with a stick, but I couldn't get 'em loose. Then the tide came in, great big waves, and I'd start sinking down in the sand, like it was bog or something. I always used to wake up just before I drowned. It was some frightening, let me tell you. And Stella, then, picking and plucking at me, bawling about how she seen the whales in her bedroom. I never knew what to say to her. Them two whales there, drowning on the beach, getting drowned by the tide coming up. I can see it so clear in me mind, it's like it's happening right in front of me. Sometimes I haves to walk on the beach. I minds once I was at the sink, peeling a few potatoes for supper. I was having a bit of fish and brewis, it was a Friday, and Jack liked a bit of fish on Friday. I felt like I had to go for a walk on the beach. I had to put down what I was doing and go right on. I never even took me apron off. I went on down the path and stood up there listening to the water, and after a while it started to rain. I remembered that night when I had the flu, when I was little, and my mother down on the beach in her nightdress, and my father having to carry her up to bed again. It's like some kind of fit, something comes over me, this queer feeling, and I got to go.

When Stella was a baby, it used to come over me, and I'd put her in the playpen and go on out, not even shut the door behind me. It was something I had to do. I come back once, and Stella was after hauling off her diaper and smearing the shit all over herself, screeching and bawling like a scalded calf. It took a whole hour to get her cleaned up so she was fit for anything. I went out another time and come back, and she was right quiet, sitting in the corner of her playpen and staring at nothing. I think she learned after the first time not to cross me. I felt kind of bad about leaving her, but I can't explain it. It was something used to come over me, and I had to do it or I'd be tormented the rest of the day with it. I made the mistake, once, of mentioning it to Doreen Slade, down to the Lions' Club, when we were making up the lists of who was going to take the tickets at the seniors' dance, and Doreen looked at me like I had horns in me head. She said that some women went a bit mental after having youngsters, and I should get the doctor to give me some nerve pills or something. I never told anyone about it after that. They all thinks I'm cracked around here anyway.

I am thinking about Sam's letter when something drops onto the carpet in my front porch. The mailman has been here and gone again, stepping sure-footed and quiet upon my stairs, and I have not heard him. I have started writing a new book, and I am immersed in it, insensible to the passage of time. I have forgotten all about my mother. I have forgotten about Uncle Joss. I am determined to excise them from my mind. I am in my masculine disguise this morning. During the night, I awoke feeling cold and sweaty, afraid of something in the bedroom that I could not see, hovering all around me like a toxin. I could not face dressing myself in anything except what I am wearing now: torn blue jeans and a flannel shirt that once belonged to my father. It is worn thin at the elbows and has been washed so often that it is as soft as chamois. It is cold and raining outside, barely weeks past winter's last gasp. The icebergs have come down, are ranged about the coast in an eerie silence, watchful. This morning I saw the wildlife officer go past towing a bear trap on a trailer behind his pickup truck. The bears are back as well, following the seals that come down from the Arctic like the icebergs do. There is the usual spate of rubbish: bargain flyers, a newsletter from the Honourable Loyola Padraig O'Toole, Member for Conception Bay South, telling me all about his wonderful accomplishments in the House. This morning I discovered new lines fanning out from the corners of my eyes. Would Loyola be impressed by that? There is a letter addressed to me in unfamiliar masculine handwriting. I am immediately reminded of that last letter from Sam, the tiny, crabbed writing, running off the page. I force myself to wait until I've made a pot of coffee, and then I sit down at the kitchen table next to the juicy cacti in their Lean Cuisine tray and open it. It's from Sam's friend Jamie, the beautiful one, the one who is so shining and so luminous, Adonis flying out of the setting sun.

Sam is dead. More than dead, in fact; he is dead and buried. He was on a holiday to visit his grandfather in the Scottish Highlands. Grandar, he called the old man. He went out walking one evening, left the house where his grandfather lived after the old man was asleep in bed, and never returned. There was a snowstorm that night, and perhaps he got lost in it. Perhaps the wind came up and the snow blinded him and he couldn't find his way back again. Perhaps he stumbled into a hole in the bogs. Perhaps he froze to death. All of these explanations are superficial. Jamie doesn't lie very well, he is not as adept at it as I am. I could teach him how to lie successfully, how to lie in every facet of your life, so that your very existence becomes a drama.

I walk a few short steps down the hallway, pressing my palms against the wall. My hands are hot, too hot to belong to me. They should be icy cold. I find my way back to the fridge and open the freezer and rummage among the contents. I smash my way through the icing on a Sara Lee chocolate cake, gouge it with my fingers as though I were tearing holes in sanity, and stuff myself. Then I go down to the basement. There are three freezers, each one filled with things like packaged meats. I am looking for something cold, sweet and soft, something pliable that will yield to the trespass of my teeth. I find a pound of ground beef, as petrified as diamond, and thaw it in the microwave until it's soft enough for me. And then I eat it raw, like steak tartare, standing over the sink and cramming it into my mouth, the blood streaming down my chin. I am savage now, demented, I have bitten my own lip and the blood is coming down. I vomit all the meat moments after I have eaten it: great bloody clumps of ruptured flesh. I wipe my mouth carefully on the dishtowel and run the water, scraping the bits of meat into the drain. It will emerge into the bay to be eaten by fish who will take it unknowingly from my throat.

Jamie tells me about the funeral at Drumnadrochit. I have seen pictures of Drumnadrochit among my grandmother's things, and I know that it's beautiful. It's near Loch Ness, Jamie says, and sometimes in the winter this place is cold, bleak and windy, but Sam loved the Highlands because of that. I imagine that he would have loved this island, then, but I'm glad he never came here. It's better this way. I couldn't have stood it, him being so close to me, so absolutely real. I would have seen myself in him, and I'm not fitted for such scrutiny. No, it's definitely better this way.

We don't know that Sam killed himself, Stella. Jamie has been kind enough to warn me. Sorry for bringing it up like that, but it's best to be open about such things. We all fall into disrepair in this way, fashioned by our mortality. Eventually, we all descend to the earth and end as molecules, as my father ended, no more than particles, a quintessence of dust.

Early the next morning, I take all of Sam's letters and read them over, sitting by the front door with them in my lap and the spring sunshine spilling through the transom. I am looking for clues, trying to find out what we were to each other, if we were anything at all. I arrange the letters chronologically and examine them all, one by one, scrutinize his handwriting, alert for the change. I read late into the night and wake up the next day to a ringing phone and Sam's letters spread around me, clutched in my hands as if I seek somehow to cover myself with the tangible evidence of his existence. "Hello?" My own voice sounds tinny and unrealistic to me. "Hello?"

It's Uncle Joss. "Your mother is not well," he says. "She went up to see the doctor and there's a lump in her breast." He offers this to me as though expecting me to do something about it. When did he become so dependent on me? When did he start expecting my approval? He's my father; I should say something to him, something welcoming and comforting. I should tell him not to worry, but I can't. The words stick in my throat.

In the end, I tell him that I will come and see my mother on the weekend. I think I can do this, even if I have to take Liam with me. I will drive to Elsinore to see her, to put things right, to do whatever it is they both expect of me. By seducing my mother, he has insinuated himself into both our lives. He has dug himself a trench and he intends to stay, working his way deeper and deeper into my flesh like poisonous elf-shot. He's been trying to work his way into me for years.

When I was a little girl, I would go to see my father in the rooms, where he was knitting twine or repairing his nets. Sometimes Uncle Joss would be there, sitting on a barrel and smoking meditatively, talking to my father about the women of the town. My father would listen to him in a concentrated silence, nodding now and then or pausing to tap the ashes off his cigarette. Joss would mentally prepare a list of women's names and run them past my father, who would grunt or nod accordingly. I never understood this game until much later, never understood that they were gauging which of the women could be easily had. Often, Uncle Joss would take me up onto his lap and move his hips around, pressing himself into me. I remember something hard and fleshy, something that recalled for me the mysterious actions of Phineas Tuck, hid behind his mother's wood stove. He would push aside my underpants and sink his fingers into me, and I would stay absolutely still, pretending to myself that it was just a game. I somehow knew it was my part to let him do this because all uncles did this to little girls, and it was natural. He was teaching me to be a grown-up. When he was finished, he'd give me a quarter, a shiny new quarter, and tell me to go buy myself some candy. All the while this was going on, my father hummed and nodded, grunted ashes off his cigarette and knit his twine.

I tried to tell my mother about it once. I'd been lying in bed one summer night, unable to sleep because there was a bluebottle fly trapped inside the lampshade, bashing itself against the glass with a peculiar clicking sound. I kept seeing Uncle Joss as though from the wrong end of a telescope, as though he were as small as the fly, trapped inside the lampshade. I saw him and I saw myself, sitting on his lap and wearing my pink shorts, with my underpants pushed aside and his fingers in me, and finally it felt as though my eyes would burst with watching it. I got out of bed and went to the top of the stairs, where I could see my mother below me, her appearance distorted in the waves and ripples of heat rising from the wood stove, as if she were swimming underwater. I didn't understand why she had a fire in when it was so warm. I was fascinated by this image of her, shifting and rippling, flowing into the waves of heat, until finally a cinder or a knot of sap exploded inside the stove, awakening me like a handclap, rupturing my strange reverie.

I couldn't tell her what Joss did because I didn't know how to say it to her. The words were hovering there upon my tongue, an unswallowed lump; I was mute, staring at her neck with its vulnerable nape, lightly furred like the skin of peaches. What could I ever say to her? I had no language even remotely or obscurely like hers. I eventually returned to bed and slept curled up, my unspoken secret sitting at the back of my throat like a globule of filth.

I knows the way I'm going to go. I knows, now. I just heard the doctor tell me, and I knows. I got the same thing poor old Eva had, I got the cancer in me breast. I'm not going to have me titty off like she did, though — it's too late for that. The doctor said there's no need to operate, that it's gone too far. He's going to send me into St. John's to get the tests done. He wants to see if it's gone into the bone, he said. He wants to see if it's gone into the spine. I went down to the beach after I come home. Joss was gone over to Bonavista with Debbie Pottle, over to the dentist. Her mother had to go with her, Debbie's not right in the head, she's retarded, one of them Mongolian Idiots — what do they call it nowadays, Down Syndrome. She's retarded and she got to have her tooth took out, and they got to give her the gas for that because she'll go right cracked if they tries to take it out when she's awake. I went for a walk down the beach by myself. It's still a bit cold, but it's not bad, even if the ice is in. I minds the time Joss and I came here, when I was going with Jack. I don't know what I'm going to do, now. The doctor said probably three months, and that's the most. So I'll be gone by the summer. Sure, I haven't even got any money put away for me box yet or anything. And I don't know where I'm going to be buried to. Perhaps Marion might help, she's good at things like that. I'm not asking Eleanor. She wouldn't give you a drink supposing you were dying of thirst, that one.

I minds the time I seen the whales here. Was it here? Must have been. When I left Stella one evening and went down and seen 'em, two of 'em, killer whales. They were beached, and the tide was coming up. That wildlife fellow was there, but there wasn't nothing he could do. They even got that professor in to the university in St. John's to come out, but he couldn't do nothing, either. Nobody couldn't do nothing about it. They were bound and determined, now, and that was it.

I go to the Recluse Sisters in Outer Cove and ring their doorbell. I am wearing my masculine disguise, unable now to venture out without it. "I want to come in and reflect," I tell the nun who answers the door. She is little and very old and does not speak. The sisters have taken a vow of silence, but when they do speak, they speak in French. They show me into a sunny room with bowls of fresh wildflowers. There are sunbeams coming through the sheer curtains and motes of dust suspended in the air. It is early afternoon, three days after my Uncle Joss has pronounced my mother's sentence of death upon me, and I am here to consider my response. The nuns leave a jug of water and a glass upon the sideboard and, smiling, whisper away on silent feet. I am alone with myself in the middle of the convent with a jug of water and a glass and my mother's impending death upon me.

After a few moments, I am aware of a heaviness centred somewhere underneath my breast bone. I can't hear anyone else moving in the house; it is as if the nuns have all moved away or died. I begin to feel uneasy about being here, sick and panicked. The room is very white, and I feel as though I am disembodied in some strange antechamber. I get up abruptly and leave, running down to where the cliffs loom out of the ocean, and I take great, ragged lungfuls of fresh air until I am myself again.

I should have never come here, I should not have thought that I could go about the world like normal people, that I could move among them and be safe. I can't even speak of this distress, spawned from someplace inside of me, some God-knows-where. If I try to say anything about it, it will rise up out of its hiding place, fill my throat like blood or savaged flesh, and choke me. After Uncle Joss had done it to me he would slide me off his lap, and I would go along my way to spend the money he had given me. I suppose this is a kind of prostitution.

It's a real big lump. I knew that right away, as soon as I felt it, I knew it was a real big lump. And right loose, too, floating there like an eyeball, like one of those trick eyeballs you'd put in someone's drink at Halloween as a joke. It's the size of a peppermint knob, them Purity peppermint knobs that poor old Mr. Goulding used to like to suck on. I could feel more of 'em, too, up in my armpit and up in the front of my chest. I knows its gone right through me, like it went through poor old Eva. I knows I'm going to go that way, in the end.

I had to get Joss to take me up to the cottage hospital right away. I couldn't bide with it, couldn't sleep with it there in my chest like that. No sense in trying to go to bed and rest. I knew it was cancer. They says you always knows, even before they tells ye. I had to try and put some clothes on meself. Here I was in me nylon nightie that I had on. I ended up hauling a skirt and top over me nightie and then had to take the whole works off again because me legs weren't shaved. And Joss out in the car, then, revving the motor like he does, hitting the gas pedal until I nearly went off me head. He only does it because he knows it gets on me nerves.

The doctor was some young, like that one me mother sees in town — a fellow from South Africa, one of them Boers or whatever it is they calls 'em now. He was right tall and skinny, with red hair and eyelashes so light you couldn't even see 'em. The nurse gave me one of them paper hospital gowns to wear and told me to lie down on the bed, and then she covered me up with a paper sheet. I knowed who she was, it was that Judy Browne from over to Elliston, that one that left her husband and lives with this other woman down to Bonavista. "You just lie down there now, Missus, and the doctor won't be too long." She forgets that I knew her mother — went to school with her, sure. Eileen Drodge she was then, before she married Fred Browne. She had real big tits, and the boys used to tease her all the time, and she'd get right red in the face about it.

The doctor had cold hands, and he never looked at me face the whole time, not once. He felt the lump and moved it around, and then felt up in me armpits and me neck, and then he sighed and went away. He never even said one word to me, look. Would it have killed him to say hello or goodbye or kiss me arse? Some people got no manners. And then Judy Browne comes back in and says they wants to do a biopsy, but I got to have that done in St. John's, because they don't do them at the cottage hospital. Awful lot of frigging around, if you asks me. Sure, I knows I got cancer. I knows I'm going to end up like poor old Eva. There's no sense pretending about it. It's just as well to face up to the truth, sure.

I am digging in my garden when the phone rings. I start up, bolt for the back door, which seems to shrink in width so that I strike my shoulder off the frame. I snatch the phone in time to prevent the call from vanishing. It's Uncle Joss, he's calling from the Health Sciences Centre. He says my mother has been admitted to the hospital and can I bring her the things she needs? A clean nightie, underpants, talcum powder. He says this as if he expects me to go out and shop for them, bring them to him in a wheelbarrow. I allow the silence between us to grow and linger, becoming larger and larger while he hunts around for something to say. I refuse to fill the gap for him. I refuse to make it easy. I ask him for the room number. "What do you need that for?" he asks. I tell him I need the number of my mother's hospital room so the taxi driver will know where to bring the parcel. He is incredulous when I tell him I will not be coming. He pretends this is some huge, portentous decision. "Sure, she's your mother. Aren't you going to see her?"

I am seized with a fit of shaking, and I depress the switch hook quickly, lay the receiver down. I can no longer hold it back, this venom that bubbles up inside of me. If he were here in person, I would claw his eyes out; I would cheerfully cut his throat.

In the end, I decide to go. I tell myself it's because I'm curious. I have never seen the dying this close. I cannot deny myself this vision.

CHAPTER TEN

My mother is in a room that isn't a room but a ward, but there's no one occupying the three other beds. She has this empty space all to herself, and I'm sure she likes it. Her window faces the parking lot, the great incinerator stack, the wooded hills behind the hospital. I can see tiny people getting into tiny cars, holding imaginary conversations.

My mother's bed is empty when I arrive. The television set is on, but there's no sound coming from it. When I pick up the earphones and fit them to my ears, I can hear the sounds of whale song. It's a program on the Discovery Channel about killer whales. I don't understand why my mother is watching it.

The room has the same disgusting antiseptic smell that everyone expects, that everyone expects and talks about. A man outside the door is speaking, and for a moment he sounds just like Sam, and I am paralyzed. But then I see him passing by, a doctor who looks nothing like Sam, and I am relieved. I couldn't stand to be haunted by him, by anyone. The television program is showing two orcas as they beach themselves, gliding ashore with weightless ease, settling into the cold, damp sand. I lay down the parcel containing a new nightie, a package of socks, two packages of underpants, and a tin of talcum powder, and I leave the room. When I walk back through the hallways and sink down in the elevator, it is as though I am being swallowed up by something, and I'm glad. In the elevator, all alone, I feel comforted and safe. It's a good thing to be devoured.

When I first woke up, my arms was some sore. They took both me breasts off, even though it's no use at all to me. I knows I'm going to end up like poor old Eva. But no, the doctor said that if they took me titties off, I might have a chance. I don't care what they does with me, to tell the truth. I don't give a jesus. They took the whole works: the breasts, the muscles underneath, the nodes. I took the bandages off this morning to have a look at it, and it's all red and raw like meat. It don't hurt. It's only me arms that hurts me. The rest of it don't feel like nothing at all.

I had a queer dream when I was under, when they give me the gas. I was back home in Elsinore, lying on the beach where Joss got me with Stella. I felt like there was a rock on me, and I couldn't breathe, and I knew in the dream that if I could get back in the water I'd survive. I could live if I got back in the water, only it felt like all the air was pressing out of me lungs. I could hear the water roaring behind me, and I wanted to turn around and go to it, but I couldn't move. And then I heard the nurse calling to me: "Mrs. Goulding, Mrs. Goulding," and I wondered who she was talking to. "My name is Minerva Bristow," I told her, and she just laughed. I think they hears a lot of silliness when people is coming out from under the gas like that. I started singing this song I minds my father singing years ago when my mother was in the San, and then I must have drifted off to sleep, because when I come to meself, Joss was in the room with the doctor and the two of 'em were talking. I knows they were talking about me.

Well, it's all gone through me. I knew that. I could have told you that, anyway. It's in the lymph nodes, the doctor said, it can go anywhere from here, it's gone right through me whole system. It's just a matter of where it appears to first — could be in my brain, in the bone, in the spine. He says all this just like it's nothing to him, right offhanded. He don't care about me at all. He'll go out of here and get in the elevator with his friends and go down and eat Tim Hortons in the cafeteria. He'll laugh about it when he's eating kangaroo at some restaurant down on Water Street. You can get kangaroo in St. John's, you know, have it cooked and brought right to your table, although I don't think it's fit to eat, myself. But you can get it at a restaurant downtown. Kangaroo and wild boar and hedgehogs and all that queer old stuff.

"Someone will be up later to discuss chemotherapy with you." The doctor says this as he's going out the door. He got five or six more like me to tend to, five or six more on this floor alone, women. He must get sick of seeing 'em. He probably don't remember faces anymore, only the tits he takes off. As soon as he's gone I tells Joss I'm going to check myself out. I don't want none of that. I don't see no need of drawing it out like that. I tells Joss to get the car and meet me at the front door. I wants to go on home out of it. That's the only thing I wants.

Liam e-mails me an image of the new book's cover, the one with the picture of the young man on it. I like the way he looks, gazing out at nothing, his one blue eye and one brown eye appearing to glance in different directions. He sees everything at once and nothing at all. He is like me.

There are regular letters from Jamie. I don't understand why, I've done nothing to encourage him. I wonder if he thinks I'm some kind of surrogate for Sam, that I can replace Sam. Perhaps he wants the comfort of someone who was close to Sam, albeit without physical connection. Ours was a relationship remarkable for its remoteness, and I liked it that way. There was no messiness, nothing that might rub off, no sticky trails. We were each of us confined in our separate boxes, contained.

Spring has ripened into summer, a tentative Newfoundland summer, with tiny buds at the ends of branches and slender stalks of grass overtaking the back yard. I put up a hammock, string it between the two large maples that border my fence, and lie there boneless for hours at a time, swinging in the breeze as though I had been hanged. I listen to the phone ringing through the open patio door and revel in the fact that I am able to ignore it now. It can only be my mother or Uncle Joss, calling to apprise me of her deteriorating condition. I can't stand to hear that kind of anguish; I have plenty of my own. I have Jamie to worry about, and his constant letters and phone calls. I think about having my phone number changed, but I vacillate for days, wondering whether I am happy to hear from him or not. He intimidates me far more than Sam ever did. He is too beautiful for me to see him properly. And yet I maintain this link to him because he is all that I have left of Sam. As such, there is nothing more between us than a courtesy. He is seven years younger than I am, and I could never have any sort of relationship with him. It would be like giving myself an incredibly extravagant and wasteful gift, something I didn't deserve and wasn't worthy of. Part of me likes to think he's fallen in love with me, even as I try to reconcile precisely what kind of relationship he had with Sam. Probably best friends, guy pals with an interest in dog racing and the football, drinking lots of beer on weekends and getting legless. Jamie isn't married, either, so it would be convenient, and they could have each other's company without having to answer for it, to anyone.

I go out and rent all of Jamie's movies and watch them late at night, when I am most alone. I see him in some period piece, as an eighteenth-century naval officer, and I think about how easily he fits into that — or any — milieu. I sense that the gap between us can never be bridged, and that he conceives of me as a very potent relic, something bottled in formaldehyde and set upon a shelf, suspended and absolutely other. Besides which, I am thoroughly sick of love or any kind of human affection — I've made that mistake. A few years ago, when I was still very much in the world, there was a Lithuanian poet who flattered me with words and caressed me with his poesy so I would do his laundry for him, type his university papers, drive him here and there in lieu of taxis and at my own expense. He only ever paid me in poems and lamentations, scraps of oddness written on matchbooks.

I will not allow Jamie to get any closer to me than letters. I can't afford it.

I've had Joss calling her for three days. I wants to speak to her. I knows I don't have much time left. I knows me time is getting short. I wants to talk to her, but I can't get hold to her. Joss is gone into St. John's to pick up Marcella O'Brien from her daughter's house. I told en to stop by in Topsail and get hold to Stella. I wants to talk to her. She's me daughter, after all.

I finds it hard to breathe nowadays. I gets Joss to take me out onto the porch on the front of the house when the weather is warm. I likes to look at the flowers. When we found out I didn't have very much time left, he went over to Bonavista and got some flowers to put in, all different kinds: geraniums, marigolds, pansies, petunias and a bunch of other ones I don't know the names of. He spent every evening putting 'em in the ground, all around the front of the house, so I could see 'em when they bloomed. I got me headstone ordered. I had Joss call in to Muir's, in town, to get me a nice one. I don't want nobody to have to deal with that after I'm gone. And the minister was here to see me, and I told en what I wanted for me funeral, what hymns I wanted sung. I likes to have stuff straightened up ahead of time so I don't have to go worrying about it at the end. The cancer is gone into me lungs, now. That's what happens when it gets exposed to the air: it goes wild, goes right through ye. I could have told the doctor that, but he wouldn't listen to nothing I had to say. Men never listens to ye. They got to go their own way and do what they wants to do. They don't care for chick nor child.

I had a phone call from my mother last night. I don't know how she knew, because I never said nothing to her. I never said a word to her. Joss picked up the phone out in the front room and brung it in to me. "It's your mother," he said. He looked right frightened to death. "She wants to speak to ye." We got one of them new cordless phones so I don't have to get up and answer it if Joss is gone in to St. John's in the taxi or over to Bonavista. I haven't spoke to my mother in years. Not since Stella was a girl. She went into the home by herself, didn't say nothing to nobody. Just up one day and sold the whole works — the house my father built, the truck that wasn't even paid off, everything. Packed up her suitcase and checked herself into the Catholic home in St. John's, never said a word to no one. Of course, she wasn't going to say nothing to me, anyway, because we never got on with each other. I don't know what in the name of God Stella sees in her, but she was always glommed on to her when she was a youngster. You'd think my mother shit gold coins, the way Stella was always stuck around her. "I heard you're not well." This is what she says to me now, after all these years. "Ye should be in the hospital." I felt like telling her right where to go, and that's the God's honest truth.

"They can't do nothing for me. I only got a few weeks left." I should be afraid or nervous, I don't know, but I'm not. I don't know why I'm not afraid, because I keeps having that dream all the time now, that dream about being on the beach and being crushed, and I feels like I'm smothering. I wakes up in a cold sweat and haves to get Joss to help me out of bed so I can take a turn around the kitchen.

"He'll come for ye." She says this like she knows something that I don't. I think she's gone senile, meself, I think she's after getting soft in the head. "He'll come for ye, just like he come for my mother. Just like he'll come for me and for Stella when the right time comes."

I don't know what the jesus she's talking about. It's the same old foolishness she used to be getting on with when I was a youngster. She never changes, she'll never change. She'll die the way she is, and so will I. I wants Joss to get hold to Stella. I needs to talk to her. I got things I needs to say to her, things I can't say in a letter or over the phone. Things I needs to talk about. If I don't say it now, I'm never going to get another chance. I'm having trouble breathing lately, and I wakes up sometimes gasping for breath. I knows it's not going to be long and I'll be gone. I got to talk to her before it's too late.

I get up early one morning in late June and decide to walk along the trail I made. For some reason, I wake up before the sunrise, just as daylight is carving a thin slice of the horizon. I feel as though I didn't sleep, or if I did, I spent the entire night floating in some non-dream. For all this, I am curiously refreshed, ready to walk, interested in the meaning of the morning. I am some distance from my house when I stumble on him, and it's true, I literally stumble. I am in that near-trance that so often occurs when I am walking like this, and before my mind can register the thing my foot has touched, I am upon him.

He is a young man, lying face down on the ground, or at least I think he's a young man, I can't see his face. He has the lanky limbs and curiously boneless aspect of a young man, and then I catch the point of his shoulder and turn him over as though I were tumbling a sack of rags. He's not unhandsome but rather otherworldly. He looks like something that has been tossed ashore after a storm at sea, a hurricane. There's an enormous welt on his left cheek, puffed and bruised about the edges, as though someone had struck him with a blunt object, like a flatiron. There are bite marks on his lips and around his mouth, corresponding bite marks on the backs of his knuckles. For a moment, I wonder if he is afflicted by my own malady, if he enacts dramas in a sheltered spot, if he feels the need to purge himself of any and all emotion. When I raise him and speak to him, he merely stares at me dumbly, like an animal, and I wonder if he can speak or if he's beautifully mute. How fortunate, then, that I should meet him — I, who can't bear the sound of another human voice. "Who hurt you?" I ask him this, gently touching the wound on his cheek. "Who did this to you?" But he flinches from me and shakes his head; he will not answer. His eyes are two different colours, brown and blue, mismatched like stolen marbles. His skin is as pale as wax. "Will you come up to the house with me? So I can help you?" This seems to please him, for he smiles, a smile that transforms his features and brings a strange light into his mismatched eyes. I see that he is beautiful, dangerously so.

In my kitchen he allows me to take off his filthy, ragged sweater, and I see that his ribs are blackened and bruised, as though someone had kicked him. I know that, even though he will not say anything, someone has beaten this boy, and beaten him badly. I set myself a task; I tend to his wounds, washing his white, white skin and feeling as if I were handling the sacred flesh of some ancient creature. I lay out bread and cheese, a plate of cold cuts left over from last night's supper, a piece of deep-fried fish. He ignores all of it except the fish, which he eats by digging at it with his fingers, extracting tiny pieces which he slips into his mouth. He does this gracefully, as if it were something he had studied in some other place a long time ago; he doesn't eat like other people eat. I've never seen anyone consume a piece of fish the way he does, as if it were something rare and sacred, something precious. I take him to the spare bed, indicate that he must lie down and rest. I've no idea how long he's been out there, lying on the ground, wet with dew and the remnants of the summer rain. When I lean close to pull the blankets over him, I catch his scent: he smells exactly like the sea. I remember the old stories that my mother used to tell me, men and seals alike, swimming in the icy sea, men turning into seals or, casting off their skins, shifting back into the shape of men. *Gone to get a selkie skin to wrap the baby bunting in.* I wonder who has beaten him. I wonder why there are bite marks on his lips, bite marks on his hands.

When he awakens, it is dark, and a huge, gibbous moon has risen over the roof of my house. I am sitting by the open patio door, listening to a moth bashing itself against the porch light. A tape unspools slowly on the stereo: recorded whale song and various marine noises thought to be soothing by those who purport to know such things. I can't think why I'm playing this music, except I have an idea that he might like it. He has been in my presence less than a day, and already I am making these kinds of concessions. He comes to me so silently that he is at my side before I notice him. He is draped in a sheet, as though it were a skin. He doesn't speak to me; he's listening to the whale song, and in a heartbeat, in a flicker of consciousness, his left eyelid begins to droop and his mouth contorts into a savage grin. I am too slow to catch him when he falls, but I kneel beside him as the fit plays itself out, ravaging him. I cup my hand under his chin and hold his head steady; I've read somewhere that this is what you're supposed to do, even though I can't remember why. While this is happening, I'm talking to him, very slowly and very gently reciting something my grandmother used to say, or probably it was Liam — something in Gaelic, something I don't understand but which seems to soothe him. His body vibrates, and then the seizure leaves him, and he is lying on the floor, blinking up at me. I know he'll speak now. I know this new crisis must surely have freed his tongue. He lays his thumb against the centre of my forehead, just between my brows, and presses hard, as though he were pushing something through my skin. This is strange behaviour, and I wonder why I allow it, but I don't pull away from him. I stay there, kneeling over him, my hand under his chin as though I were raising him from some mystical immersion, as though we had both just been baptized.

"I'll tell you." He blinks, surprised at this sudden utterance. His voice sounds human, and I am faintly disappointed. Of course he's human. There are no selkies anymore. It's all a fairy tale. "I'll tell you some little truths about myself, or at the very least, a palatable lie. I'll tell you what I know."

"Who are you?" I help him to his feet, again surprised by the solid weight of him. Yes, he must be wholly human, because fairies can't possibly be as solid and as fleshed as this.

"My name's Edward. Edward Monk." He was in the foster care of a woman in Heart's Content, he tells me, but he is originally from Elsinore. I know immediately that I can hide nothing from him, that he will be privy to my worst secrets. He is from Elsinore; he knows the curses that cling to its soil. Doubtless he knows of my mother, of my father and Uncle Joss. He is the son of a fisherman who used to live in Elsinore but who died drunk in a snowbank the Christmas Eve when Edward was four. Edward's mother is violent, a woman who liked to beat him with a broom handle and who would play odd, seductive games with him when he was a teenager. I can imagine her as he describes her: tall and slender and very beautiful, with flaming red hair that she wears looped in braids beside her ears, like the Swiss woman on the cocoa can. "My mother is so beautiful," he says. He is sitting next to me with a chair pulled close to mine, and we are sipping Scotch out of my crystal glasses. "She's beautiful and cruel, as only beautiful women can be."

I wonder why I'm not uncomfortable in his presence; I wonder why he can tell me such intimacies and I'm not frightened. I'm never this at ease with anyone, not even Liam. Maybe I would have felt this way with Sam if he had lived. "She used to come into my bed, you know." He would wake up at night and find her hands on him, touching him as she crooned old songs and rocked against his body, seeking her release. If he awakened during these interludes, he understood that he was to stay absolutely still until she gasped and cried, until her slender thighs shivered and she slipped quietly away. He knew it was ended, then, he knew their coupling was done. "She hit me with a knife, hit me on the head. She was always hitting me." This is why the seizures come, because of the repeated beatings. He is unemotional as he tells me his story, but in the darkness near the door I think I can discern the gleam of tears upon his thick, dark lashes.

I decide to do something unprecedented, something unusual and foreign. I ask him to get dressed, and then I take him with me, lock the doors behind us, and walk the quiet midnight streets until we reach the ocean. It's quiet here, quieter than it has a right to be; everyone who lives here is in bed, and there is only the slow drone of passing vehicles, far away on the high road, speeding towards St. John's. "I don't come here anymore." I take my shoes off and wade into the icy water up to my knees; when I turn to find him he is there beside me, dark and mysterious, nearly naked in the moonlight. He is some kind of god, I know it. He has come for me because I needed him and because I want to be possessed by him. I need him in some other fashion, in some manner that I have never considered until now. When he kisses me, his mouth tastes like the sea. We are clinging to each other in the ebbing surf, my fingers digging into his waist, accidentally hurting him, touching all his bruises, this line of bruises that disappears beneath his belt like the dappling spots on a seal. For all his youth, he is entirely mature, educated in these necessary dances, and when I let him enter me there is a single bloom of pain, a bubble of blood that bursts and disperses in the foam. I am lying half in and half out of the freezing water, but I can't feel the cold. I have never been with anyone like this, and I have never been with anyone like him. My fingers re-member the shape of his naked back as though we had coupled many times before, on beaches just like this, under a similar approving moon. When it is finally over, we lie together on the warm, wet sand, our bodies trembling. He traces the contours of my face with one long finger, making small murmurs of appreciation as he does this. "I knew that you were kind," he says, "because I can see what people look like inside." Some people have a hateful orange light that comes from them, and some have lights that are all grey around the edges, but I have a hazy purple light, he says. He quotes Baudelaire to me, and John Donne, and Sir Thomas More. When we go back to the house, I invite him into my bed. We fall asleep immediately, wet and spackled with the sand, smelling of the ocean. I dream of him, striding from the waves, wrapped up in a selkie skin.

CHAPTER ELEVEN

I am with my mother, in her house in Elsinore, sitting in her kitchen now and sipping cups of tea while Uncle Joss chops wood just outside the door. I don't know why he's chopping wood, surely not to burn. It's the middle of July, it's warm now, the solstice has come and gone and summer is here. Surely my mother doesn't burn wood now, when the time for burning bonfires has come and gone. She doesn't talk as much as she used to, but I know that she's dying. She hasn't said anything, and she doesn't need to. She sits for long periods now, gazing out the kitchen window, gazing at the way the tall grass waves and bends in the wind, gazing at the patterns the clouds make across the sky. The time is getting close, and she understands this. She understands what will be expected of her. She has discussed it with her doctor, she says. She thinks she knows how it will feel, the way it will come to her. Edward is standing by a corner of the house, like a figure in a painting. He is smoking a cigarette, and I find this strange, that a creature such as he is should indulge this way. I expected I would find him holy. I expected some sort of numinous unfolding, some blessing from his presence. He has not said he loves me, and I know that I don't love him. For now he is content to stay with me while his wounds heal, until he can remember where he came from and why he needs to go back there. He is in Elsinore so that he can remember — this is what he tells me. He is standing by the corner of the house, watching Uncle Joss chop wood, but he doesn't offer to help. His blue eye watches Uncle Joss while his brown eye watches the house. Through the open kitchen window, I can hear the roaring of the sea.

"You wants to put a drop of hot water in that, warm it up. Sure, don't drink that, Stella. It's all gone cold now." My mother reaches one hand towards the teapot on the table, halts suddenly as though someone had stabbed her with a pocketknife. All her features have frozen in a rictus of pain; her eyes are filling up with it. It must be in her lungs now. It must be burning painful paths along her nerves, straight into her brain.

"I'll get it, Mother." I take the pot to the stove with me, the old wood-and-oil stove, fill it from the kettle that is always kept boiling on the back. The scent of tea curls into my nostrils, raw and wet like uncured varnish. I fill my mother's cup and slide it across the table to her. The table is covered with the same oilcloth as it was when I was a child: white, with a pattern of surrealistic fruit and strange birds perched upon slender stalks of wheat. The fruit is orange and yellow and so are the birds. The person who made the oilcloth had limited colours at his disposal, I imagine, and so was forced to make do with whatever he had. We sit like this for some time, my mother and I, not saying anything. I see Edward through the window, moving to where Uncle Joss is hacking at a piece of wood; I see the two of them talking, but I can't hear what is being said. The wind and the roar of the ocean drown out everything.

"I knows that boy," my mother says suddenly. Her voice breaks into my thoughts: I had been thinking of Edward, that night upon the sand, upon the beach. We have had many more such nights since he came to me. I will not allow myself to admit that I enjoy the feeling of his hard young body in my bed. I'm above such material concerns as this.

"How do you know Edward?" I ask her.

"I knows him. I seen him before." She nods towards the

window, and I see again the toll that her illness has taken upon her. There are pouches underneath her eyes where there were none before, and hollow shadowed places on her cheeks. Her face has fallen in upon itself. I wonder where the woman has gone, that beautiful woman that so terrified me. I think I would be more comfortable if she were to reappear, declare this whole scenario a joke, and whisk my mother's ruined body away so that I wouldn't have to look at it. "I seen him once when I was a little girl," she says. I have to look twice at her to see whether she has lost her mind. Edward is twenty years old. My mother could not possibly have seen him when she was a girl. "That night when I got up out of bed, when my mother went down on the beach. I seen en then. That's why she went down there."

"Down on our beach? On this beach?" The beach that is the terminus of the shell-littered path in front of the house, the beach that stands in stolid watch along the shore. "No, Mother. You're thinking about someone else."

"No, I'm not. You thinks I'm gone soft in the head, but I'm not, Stella." She has taken more and more to using my name, when she never did before. Where once she wanted to push me away, keep me at arm's length, now she desires to draw me close. She cannot know that I will never allow it — that her kind of love is far too dangerous for me, and I cannot afford to be devoured by her again. "I knows that boy. He was down there on the beach." And she launches into the tale about seeing her mother in her long white nightdress, dancing on the beach, and her father having to retrieve her, carrying her up the slippery seaside shingle to the house, cursing. She tells me how her mother would leave the house without provocation at any hour of the day or night and walk down to the sea, stand there staring into the horizon as if waiting for something. She followed my grandmother once and watched from behind a hillock as my grandmother knelt down on the sand and put her mouth to it, as though blowing into it or speaking into a hole in the ground. "Like she was calling someone," my mother says, "like she was talking to someone."

Edward is standing by the pile of wood; Uncle Joss is no-where in sight. The late afternoon sun is glancing off the wave tops with a brightness that is almost painful to the eyes. Edward's body is turned as though he were looking out to sea, but he isn't; Edward's body is turned towards the ocean but Edward is look-ing through the kitchen window. He is looking at my mother. "Go and get the photo albums," my mother says, as if remem-bering something long forgotten. "In my bedroom, in the box behind the door."

I rummage in the darkness for a while — my mother never opens the drapes in her bedroom anymore — until I find what I am looking for: a Purity biscuit box stacked full of old photo albums. "The big one, Stella, with the wine-coloured cover." I find it and bring it to her, wait while she pages through it, licking her finger and thumb each time she turns over a leaf, repeating this action like a physical mantra. She tells me who the people are in the pictures: here is Aunt Rhoda, just out of the Mental, her hair all done up in a bun with flowers in it, she was always half-cracked, don't know where she got that from. Here is Great-Grandmother Bristow, over in Scotland, standing on the seashore in the Outer Hebrides, a young man standing beside and slightly behind her. His hair is dark and silky-looking, like a pelt, and flows unconfined over his shoulders in the late Victorian style. He is dressed in a pair of rubber boots and dark trousers and wears a sweater knitted in some intricate pattern . . . a fisherman's sweater, a sweater to identify the body if he were to drown at sea. He is standing with his hand upon my great-grandmother's arm, and they are smiling into the camera, and even though the print is very old, I can clearly see that one of his eyes is light, the other dark.

The kitchen door opens, and Edward comes in. From out in the yard I can hear the sound of Uncle Joss, chopping wood again. He chops methodically, with a regular rhythm like the ticking of a clock. "I'm going for a walk on the beach," Edward says. My mother and I are silent.

It's time I done this and got it over with. I got everything took out of the closet, out of the bureau drawers, took all the boxes out from under the bed, and I'm going through it all. Half of it is junk, the kind of old foolishness you keeps and never throws out, thinking that some day you're going to have a use for it, but you knows yourself, you never will use it again. I got me jewellery box here, the one that Jack give to me when we was married, with all me rings and necklaces in it. I never had a real lot of good jewellery. Jack could never afford to give it to me, but he managed one time to get me this real nice necklace that he ordered out of a maga-zine, down the States. I think he got Eleanor to fill out the order form, because he couldn't read or write. But he seen the picture of the necklace and that was what he wanted, he said. It was three dolphins on a silver chain, leaping out of the water just like they were alive. You'd look at 'em in a certain kind of light and you'd swear they was swimming on the end of the chain. I was frightened to death to wear it, frightened I'd lose it. I'd never forgive meself.

I'm going through all of what I got, because there's only Stella, and I got it in me mind to leave her a little parcel of things to re-member me by: a few pairs of earrings, a watch that belonged to my mother, things like that. I'm going to keep the dolphin neck-lace, I wants to be buried in that. I don't know why. Jack give it to me, and I don't know why I wants to keep it, but I do. I'm going to keep the dress, too, the blue dress, and I'll give that to Joss. He'll need to burn that down on the beach when I'm gone. But I wants to give Stella something. My mother never gave me nothing.

There's someone in the house. No, it can't be. I must be dream-ing it, sure. I think I'll go and see if there's someone at the door. Maybe Joss is back early. Maybe he forgot something and had to come back for it. I can find me own way out to the front door. Probably I forgot to latch it like Joss always tells me to. I forgets to latch it, and then the wind takes it and it bangs all night. It always smells like the salt water in this kitchen. I don't know what it is. Perhaps the house is built too close to the beach. Perhaps that's what's wrong with it, it's too close to the water, and maybe the water is after coming up from the ground and seeping into the foun-dations. I must ask Joss about that when he comes back. Men knows about stuff like that. But it's some cold, it's right cold, like in October when you gets the cold wind from off the water. It's not supposed to be cold like that yet, not yet. It's not supposed to be. I must check the door, make sure the wind haven't took it.

I'm not surprised it's him. I knowed it would be him. I knows it's time for me to go along with him. I'm not afraid of en at all. I seen en before, when I was little. My mother seen en, too, and now Stella knows en. "Let me get the dress," I says, "so's Joss can burn it on the beach." That's what you got to do with the skin, after it's over with, you got to burn it, so the Devil can't come back and get what's his. I minds me mother telling about it when I was a little girl. *Always take the skin with ye, so they can't get it.* "Let me go in the other room and get the dress." But he's hanging onto me, now, and my God, his hands are cold, his hands are right cold. He looks just the same as that day Stella brought him here. He looks the same as in the picture in the album. They don't get old like we do, they don't age the same way people do. Me grandmother used to say it had something to do with the cold water, the cold water slowed 'em down inside, so they wouldn't age like people do. He won't say nothing to me. I minds my mother telling me about it, how they never says anything, just takes you along with 'em. I feels like I should get dressed up proper, sure, I'm only in me nightdress, but no, he wants me to come with en. The only thing to do is go. That's all I knows.

It begins with the dream, as a forecast of my mother's death. I am walking back in the old road, the one leading to our house in Elsinore, when I meet a group of mourners who say they are going to see my mother. In a great flood of tears I proclaim, "Mother is dead." The dream ends the way all unsettling dreams do, and I awaken, blinking in the pale light of the early dawn, feeling disembodied, surreal and alone. But I am not alone. No, I am never alone. I reach across the bed to touch his sleeping shoulder, reassure myself of him, the coolness of his body, the scent of him, the smell of lashing waves. "When I was a boy in Armagh," he says, "I always had bad dreams: that I was drowning on the ocean, lost alone at sea." He understands this kind of sorrow because he is so steadfast. He understands that nothing can be undone, and all of it — my mother, Uncle Joss, the man who was my father — all of it is transitory, ephemeral and brief. He understands that we must embrace the evidence of our own mortality.

This is the quietus that we make.